GILGAMESH OF URUK

Tamara Agha-Jaffar

© 2018 Tamara Agha-Jaffar. All Rights Reserved.
No part of this book may be reproduced in any form or by any electronic or mechanical means, including information storage and retrieval systems, without permission in writing from the author, except by a reviewer, who may quote brief passages for review.

Cover image: Detail of Representation of Gilgamesh, the king-hero from the City of Uruk, battling the 'bull of heavens'; terracotta relief kept at the Royal Museums of Art and History, Brussels. 10 December, 2015. By U0045269 [Public domain or CC BY-SA 4.0 (https://creativecommons.org/licenses/by-sa/4.0)], from Wikimedia Commons.

Cover design by Rebekkah Dreskin
www.blameitonrebekkah.com

To Yasin and Ayah

Chapter 1: The Opening

She looked out at the ocean, shielding her eyes from the unrelenting sun. From where she stood in her home, her home of many decades, she could hear the waves gently lapping the shore. The waters look so mild and gentle, she thought. But looks were deceptive. The Waters of Death. She knew one drop of that seemingly mild and gentle water would send a person plummeting to the netherworld. Not even she or Utnapishtim could touch the water without facing the consequences.

They lived alone, isolated. Their only visitor was Urshanabi, the ferryman. The gods allowed him to cross the Waters of Death to ferry their supplies. But even he had to be vigilant when he made the journey. He couldn't cross the Waters of Death without the Stone Men to row his boat. Only they were able to touch the waters unscathed. The gods forbade Urshanabi to bring anyone else on the island. No visitors at all, they commanded. They were very clear about that. Utnapishtim and Old Woman were to live alone on Dilmun for all eternity. Absolutely no visitors allowed. It had been that way for many years—more years than anyone could remember.

She sighed.

She looked across at her husband, Utnapishtim, slouched on his favorite chair. His eyelids were getting heavy, his breathing rhythmic. He was about ready to doze off. Their forever life didn't seem to bother him as much as it bothered her. Is this what it's going to be like forever and ever? she thought. How long can we go on like this? But she already knew the answer. She knew there was no point in asking the question. It was a gift of the gods. She shrugged. Some may call it a gift. She called it a curse. What kind of gift ages your body without giving you the release of death? What kind of gift haunts you with memories you'd rather forget? A gift, indeed!

Utnapishtim would get angry with her when she spoke those thoughts aloud. We're the only mortals to receive this precious gift from the gods, he always reminded her. He would shush her, afraid the gods would overhear. Let them overhear, she would say defiantly. What will they do to me? Kill me off? Send me to the netherworld? Better than this, she would argue. Better than living forever.

He called it a gift. She called it a curse.

The gods had settled them on this island of Dilmun after Enlil granted them eternal life. Alone on the island. Urshanabi would occasionally ferry the god Shamash to Dilmun to see how they were getting along. Utnapishtim would get very nervous whenever Shamash showed up. He was afraid she would say something to offend the god. He was afraid she might get into one of her moods and blurt out she didn't want this so-called gift any more. But she never said anything when the god was around. She knew better. She had learned when to keep her mouth shut and when it was acceptable to speak.

The visits of Shamash always put a strain on them. Utnapishtim would try to convince her they should be honored. After all, Shamash, the sun god, didn't come very often. But when he did come, they had to be on their best behavior. Put on a show.

As she looked at her husband dozing off in his chair, Old Woman recalled Shamash's last visit. Utnapishtim's hands shook. His voice quivered as he tried to say and do the right thing to please the god. Fortunately, she was always ignored on these visits, practically invisible. She preferred it that way. She cooked a sumptuous feast for the god, serving him with food and wine. She wasn't expected to speak or have an opinion. She stood silently in the corner, ready to serve, ready to refill cups, ready to clear away food when the god had finished.

She looked down at her skeletal hands. I'm getting so old, she thought, watching her fingers twitch. She didn't know how old. She was old enough to feel her bones brittling, her muscles aching, her fingers trembling. She couldn't even remember her name she was that old. Or maybe no one thought she would ever be important enough to be given a name. She shrugged. She was known as the wife of Utnapishtim the Faraway. He has called her Wife or Old Woman for so long she didn't think even he could remember her real name. She must have had a name before she married him. Maybe. Maybe, not. Urshanabi called her Mother even though she wasn't his mother. She was no one's mother anymore. She smiled, looking down at her husband as he began to snore softly.

She turned her gaze back to the ocean. She saw a speck of something bobbing in the waters. She squinted and focused. Yes, it was a boat. Urshanabi coming to pay us a visit, she thought. But there was something wrong. She looked again, rubbing her eyes. This can't be right, she thought. Was that someone with him on the boat? She rubbed her eyes even harder and looked, again. Yes, there was definitely someone with him. It wasn't Shamash. And the Stone Men were nowhere to be seen. How can that be? The Stone Men were the only ones who could touch the Waters of Death without paying for it with their lives. She scrunched up her eyes and looked again. She raised her voice in a panic.

"Husband! Husband! Wake up! Utnapishtim, wake up!"

He waddled in his chair, groaning softly.

"Wake up, Utnapishtim! Wake up!" she shouted.

"Huh? What? I'm right here, Old Woman. Stop your shouting. What do you want? I'm trying to take a nap. Leave me alone."

"Come quickly. Come and see."

"Come and see what? What is it? Whatever it is, can't it wait? I'm tired."

"No. You have to come now. Come quickly."

"All right. All right. I'm coming." He reached out for his cane and pulled himself up gingerly. He took a minute to settle himself before hobbling toward the sound of her voice, grunting and puffing.

"It's always something," he mumbled in irritation under his breath. Years of living together had taught him it was useless to argue with her. "This better be good, Wife," he grumbled. "What do you want?"

He shuffled toward her. She followed his eyes as they traced the signs of aging up and down her body. A wrinkled, leathery face burnt from the sun. Brown spots covering weathered hands. Wisps of thin, white hair peeking from under a headscarf. A back bent with age. Yes, she was old. But her eyes were as sharp as ever. They didn't miss a thing.

"Look." Her gnarled fingers pointed toward the waters.

"What is it?" His eyesight was not what it once used to be.

"It's a boat."

"Huh? A boat? Is that all? You woke me up just for that? You've never seen a boat before? It's only Urshanabi coming to pay us a visit. Nothing unusual about that."

"Look, again, old man." Irritation mounted in her voice. "Of course, I've seen a boat. And I know Urshanabi's boat when I see it. But that's not what I'm talking about. There's someone with him. And it's not the Stone Men who ferry him across."

"Huh? What? That's impossible! Your eyes are playing tricks on you, Old Woman. Urshanabi can't come here without the Stone Men. Only they can ferry across the Waters of Death without injury." His breathing was labored, his tone emphatic. "Everyone else would die on the spot should even a drop of water touch them. You know that as well as I do. Look again carefully. Are you sure you're seeing right?" His wrinkled brow tensed into a frown.

"Yes, of course I'm sure, you silly old fool. There's someone with him and it's not the Stone Men."

She stared into his face, defying him to challenge her. Her eyesight was better than his. She knew it. So did he.

"But how can that be?" Utnapishtim looked perplexed. "How can Urshanabi make it here without them? And who is that with him? No mortal is allowed to come here other than Urshanabi. What's going on?"

His eyes searched her face, half expecting her to provide answers. But she had no answers to give. She shrugged her shoulders. She sighed.

"Who knows? Maybe this is some trick played on us by the gods." The smirk on her face was unmistakable.

Utnapishtim scowled but said nothing. He didn't like it when she showed disrespect to the gods. He shaded his eyes against the glint of the sun. He stared long and hard at the sea, trying to will the picture into focus. The shimmering pool clouded his vision. He focused intently as his eyesight grew accustomed to the bright sunlight. She stared, too. The boat drew closer, and with its nearness, familiar forms emerged.

Utnapishtim recognized Urshanabi's boat by its color and shape. He identified Urshanabi by his long, white flowing robe. He squinted. Sure enough, there was someone else with him on the boat. She was right. The old woman was right, after all. It wasn't the Stone Men.

"This can't be," he said, turning to face her, a bewildered scowl on his face. "Urshanabi knows better than to bring someone here. How did he get here without the Stone Men? What's he up to? And who's that with him? He knows the gods won't allow anyone else here. He'd better have a good reason for doing this. He's going to get us all into trouble. The gods won't like this. No, they won't like this at all."

He rattled off his words with clenched fists, muscles taut with tension. He searched her face for answers. She had none to give, brushing his questions off with another shrug of her shoulders.

"I should go down to the shore and find out what's going on," he said through clenched teeth. "You better stay here and wait for me. There may be trouble."

She stifled a laugh. As if he with his old bones could protect her from anything or anyone! But she didn't say a word. It was best not to remind him of his aging body.

"Be careful," she said. "Take your time getting down there. You don't want to fall. I can come with you. Are you sure you don't want me to come with you?"

"Yes, I'm sure. Do as I say, Wife. For once in your life, just do as I say. Stay where you are. I have to find out what Urshanabi is up to by bringing a stranger to our shore. He's defied the gods. They won't like this. I'm telling you there's going to be trouble. And I don't want you down there until I know what's going on."

He brushed her aside and stepped out on to the warm sand. The bright glare of the sun dazzled him momentarily as he gripped his cane for support. He steadied himself before taking a step. She watched him hobble along as he made his way gingerly down to the shore, leaning heavily on his trusty cane. His back was bent with age. His white hair cascaded down to his shoulders. He was old. They were both old.

Once again, she remembered the bittersweet gift of the gods. It was never far from her thoughts. It flashed in her mind as it had done many times before. They were told it was a gift, but was it really a gift or a curse? How can it be a gift when it so often felt like a curse? The older she got, the more convinced she became that to grow old without the release of death was a curse. To grow old without being able to erase all those horrific memories could hardly be called a gift.

"If I had to do it over again," she muttered to no one there. Her thoughts trailed into the distance. She sighed as she watched Utnapishtim shuffling down the hill toward the seashore.

Chapter 2: The Visitor

Utnapishtim trod with deliberate steps to avoid the small stones and jagged rocks lining the shore. He was being extra vigilant.

"I have to avoid stumbling or I'll look very foolish," he muttered aloud to himself. He shook his head repeatedly while walking. "There had better be a good explanation for this."

He often talked to himself, especially when upset or anxious. It was a habit he had developed while still a young man, a habit that became more pronounced with age, much to the amusement of his wife. As she watched him hobbling down to the shore, Old Woman knew he was talking aloud to himself again. He supported himself with the cane in one hand and gesticulated wildly with the other, a sure sign he was talking to himself. I wouldn't want to be in Urshanabi's sandals right now, she thought. He'd better have a good explanation for this. Utnapishtim was right. The gods won't be pleased.

Utnapishtim slowly made his way to the shore and waited for the boat, anxious to hear the explanation for this unwarranted intrusion. But he was determined not to appear too apprehensive.

"Stay calm," he mumbled aloud to himself. He took several long, deep breaths. "You have all the time in the world to get to the bottom of this. The gods will know this isn't your doing. They won't blame you for this. Just stay calm," he reminded himself.

The closer the boat got, the better he could distinguish its two passengers. Urshanabi was there, his face taut with anxiety. He had someone with him. At first look, Utnapishtim thought the passenger was an old man like himself. But as the boat got closer, Utnapishtim could see the passenger was quite young.

GILGAMESH OF URUK

Clothed in animal skins with a body and face covered in filth, the young man looked dejected, haggard, forlorn, and emaciated, as if the vitality of youth had been sucked right out of him. The more Utnapishtim examined the passenger, the angrier he became. "How dare Urshanabi bring this filthy human being to my island!" he mumbled under his breath.

"What is going on, Urshanabi?" Utnapishtim shouted when the passengers were close enough to hear him. He thumped his cane on a nearby rock, demanding an answer. "Who is this stranger?" Thump, thump, thump went the cane in a series of regular beats. "Why have you brought him here? Do the gods know about this? Where are the Stone Men who help you ferry the boat? How could you come here without them? Why did you bring this man here? I've never seen him before. Who is he? Why have you brought him here?" His questions fired out in rapid succession.

Urshanabi lowered his eyes in fear and embarrassment. He tried to stitch words together, words to explain the situation. But no words would come. He remained sullen and unresponsive.

The stranger had no such misgivings. He was not at a loss for words. As soon as they were close to the shore, the young man leapt out of the boat and confronted Utnapishtim. He ignored the barrage of questions aimed at Urshanabi. He had questions of his own to ask.

"Old man," he said. "Do you know where I can find Utnapishtim the Faraway? I must speak with him. Where is he? He's been granted eternal life by the gods. I must speak with him to find out how he did it. How did he cheat death? I demand you take me to him right away."

Utnapishtim fixed his eyes on the stranger. He took an immediate dislike to him. What arrogance! he thought. How dare he question me? How dare he use that tone of voice with me? How dare he come barging on to my island and think he can order me around? He ignored the young man's questions and looked straight past him. He glared at Urshanabi.

Urshanabi remained silent, his face ashen, his lips trembling. He looked down at his sandals to avert Utnapishtim's gaze. He knew he had done wrong. But he had had no choice. This stranger, part man, part god, had already killed the Stone Men. He had even threatened to kill him unless he agreed to ferry him across the Waters of Death. But how to explain it to Utnapishtim? Would he be able to find the right words? Would he be given a chance to explain? Would Utnapishtim believe him? He continued to look down at his sandals, shuffling the dirt under his feet.

Utnapishtim cast a piercing look in Urshanabi's direction to convey his anger. He would deal with him later. He turned his attention to the stranger. He had to find out who he was and why he had come. He shook his head in dismay. The gods are going to be so angry, he thought. He turned to examine the stranger closely.

The young man's dark, shoulder-length hair was tangled and unkempt. His long beard was speckled with pieces of what looked like remnants of food and flecks of dirt. His skin was a sickly shade of olive. Utnapishtim concluded the young man did not look well. Perhaps he's ill or has suffered a misfortune, he thought. Although at the prime of his manhood, he looked aged, weary, and grief-stricken.

"Who are you?" he asked the stranger, his voice tense with displeasure. "Why have you come here? You should not have come. This is a sacred place designated by the gods. You can't just force your way in here as if you own the place, barking orders and demanding answers. Your presence here will offend the gods. You come here with your filthy hair, clothed in your filthy animal skins. The gods are not going to be pleased. You'll get us all in trouble. Who are you that you think you can get away with doing this?"

The stranger's posture shriveled up as if all the air had been sucked out of him. He bowed his head, looking downcast and dejected. His forlorn appearance stirred Utnapishtim's heart, moving him to adopt a more conciliatory tone.

"You must have been on a long journey, son. You look about ready to collapse," he said, his voice softening. "You seem devastated, grief-stricken. Are you ill? Is that why you've come? What are you doing here? Why have you come?" He repeated his questions, this time in a gentler tone.

The stranger's reply took him by surprise.

"Why shouldn't I be devastated?" he said. "Why shouldn't I be grief-stricken? I'm sad. My heart bursts with sorrow."

The young man swallowed hard, trying to suppress tears. And then, to the amazement of the two people on either side of him, he buried his face in his hands and collapsed in a fit of weeping. Tears streamed down his face, rounding into small puddles on the sand.

Utnapishtim stepped back in astonishment. He stared at the stranger in silence. He cast a bewildered look at Urshanabi as if to suggest why have you brought this blubbering young man to me? What am I to do with him? Urshanabi shrugged his shoulders. He, too, was at a loss.

"I have come a long way. I'm weary. My journey was long. I'm tired. I'm tired of weeping." The stranger sobbed, his words punctuated with gasps for breath. "My dearest friend and brother. My closest companion. He went everywhere I went. He fought by my side at every danger. He was my friend. I loved him like I have loved no other. My beloved Enkidu is dead. He is dead.

He has suffered the fate of all mankind. He is dead. My beloved is dead," moaned the stranger. And he released a primal wail from the pit of his stomach.

Utnapishtim stared in silence. He didn't know what to do. He should say something to comfort the stranger, but what should he say? Old Woman had always been more adept at handling emotional outbursts. He usually left such matters to her. He wished she were by his side now to soothe the young man. She would know what to say. He glanced back to see if she had defied his orders and followed him to the shore. She seldom paid much heed to his demands, anyway. He hoped this would be one of those times. But there was no sign of her. Of all the time in the world for her to do as I say, he thought grudgingly. He shot a frustrated look at Urshanabi and waited.

"I couldn't do it. I couldn't let him go." The young man spoke, choking back tears. "For six days, I held on to his lifeless body. I refused to give him up. I wouldn't let them bury him. I clung to him. I thought if my grief was strong enough, I might be able to bring him back," he said. "I mourned him for six days and seven nights. And then I saw it. A maggot crawling out of his nose. It was awful, just awful." He shivered. "A maggot . . . creeping out of his nose. I was frightened—frightened that I, too, will die one day and maggots will crawl in and out of my nose. Crawl all over my corpse. Just like him. Just like my beloved Enkidu."

He shivered, pausing to catch his breath. Utnapishtim remained quiet, his head bowed. He waited for the young man to compose himself.

"I am he," the stranger announced. He puffed his chest, took a deep breath, and spoke with increased composure. He raised his head and looked Utnapishtim in the eye.

"I am the king. I am Gilgamesh, King of Uruk," he said, pounding his right hand over his chest. "I am part man, part god. I have wandered in the wilderness, lost in my grief. My beloved Enkidu has been snatched from me. He has been turned into dust. And will that be my fate, too? Am I turn to dust like my beloved Enkidu, never to rise again?" He stifled a sob. "That's why I must find Utnapishtim the Faraway. He was granted eternal life by the gods. I must speak with him. I must find out how he overcame death." He paused to catch his breath.

"I'm weary," he said. "I've climbed mountains, trudged deserts, sailed the ocean. All to speak with Utnapishtim. It's been a long journey. It's been a difficult journey. I've had to overcome many perils. I've not slept in days. My body aches. I've killed animals. I've eaten their flesh. I've clothed myself in their skins. What do I have to show for it? Nothing! Not a thing! I am worn out. My body aches. My heart is broken."

Utnapishtim shook his head.

"And you made this journey because you want to speak with Utnapishtim the Faraway? You've come all this way looking for Utnapishtim?"

"Yes. I must speak to him. I must learn what happened. I want to know how he cheated death."

"Why? What good will that do you?"

"That's none of your business, old man," Gilgamesh snapped. "Just tell me where I can find Utnapishtim."

"Tell me, son. Have you come all this way thinking you can share in Utnapishtim's good fortune?" Utnapishtim tried to sound compassionate but his words were tinged with amusement. "Do you think you can wrench eternal life for yourself from the gods? You think by talking to Utnapishtim and hearing his tale, you, too, will be granted eternal life? Is that what you think?" Utnapishtim didn't conceal the smirk on his face.

"Old man, that's none of your business. Just take me to him," Gilgamesh said, his impatience growing.

"Well, my dear boy, I hate to be the one to give you the news, but you're woefully misguided." Utnapishtim sighed. "Whoever told you that you can share in Utnapishtim's eternal life deceived you. You've wasted your time. It doesn't work that way. The gods are not liberal in bestowing their gift of eternal life. They select whom they will to receive their gift. There's nothing any of us can do to change that."

"That may be so," Gilgamesh said, his voice gruff. "But I must hear it from Utnapishtim. I didn't come all this way to hear his story from a foolish old man. I must find Utnapishtim and hear his story from his own mouth. I want to know how he cheated death. Tell me at once where I can find him or . . ."

"Or what?" Utnapishtim asked, amused.

"Or you'll be sorry," Gilgamesh said.

"Really?" Utnapishtim raised his eyebrows. "You not only come here uninvited, now you think you can threaten me? I don't scare easily, son. Before you blurt out any more stupid threats and make an even bigger fool of yourself, you need to stop and think for a minute. I want you to listen to my words, son. I'm trying to help you. Have you ever considered your good fortune? I wonder if you have. I wonder if you appreciate who you are, son. You say you are Gilgamesh. You say you are part god, part human. If so, you have the blood of gods and humans coursing through your veins."

"So?" Gilgamesh interrupted. "What am I supposed to do with that? My Enkidu is dead. That's all I know. That's all I can think of. I'm going to die, too, unless I can speak with Utnapishtim."

"The gods chose you to be a ruler of men," Utnapishtim continued, ignoring the interruption. "They no doubt showered you with gifts. They gave you clothing fit for gods while your subjects dress in rags. They gave you food and drink fit for gods while your subjects feed on crumbs. Can you not be thankful for what you've received? Why do you seek something you can never have? You've journeyed all the way out here in search of a goal that will never be granted to you. You've worn yourself out. You'll accomplish nothing. Go back, son. Go home. Live your life. Your time will come soon enough. Enjoy life while you still have breath left in your body."

Utnapishtim paused to let his words register.

"Son, believe me when I tell you this, for I speak the truth. This is the way the world has worked ever since the beginning of time. The gods are in charge. They're eternal. They watch us. They never sleep. They never die. Yes, they took Enkidu from you, but whose life haven't they taken? Death eventually takes us all—young and old alike, man and woman alike."

"But not so Utnapishtim. He cheated death and will live forever," interrupted the stranger.

"Yes, but he's the exception, isn't he? Can't you see that? How many Utnapishtims are there in the world? How many? Only one. Death comes to the rest of us. It fastens its grip on us even when we're not expecting it, cutting our lives short in an instant. And yet we behave as if we'll live forever, building homes, fighting over pittances, forging allegiances, plotting against our enemies. Meanwhile, time never ceases to move forward, eventually carrying us in its wake. The dead and the sleeper may look alike, but whereas the sleeper wakes up, the dead man does not. Who knows when death will come? Only the gods know. They decide on your life and they've fixed the time of your death. But when that time will be is a secret known only to the gods. It is a secret they'll not reveal to anyone—not even to you."

"Enough of your talk, old man," Gilgamesh said, scowling. "You're wasting my time. You're not telling me something I haven't heard before. I have to speak to Utnapishtim the Faraway. I want to know how he cheated death. I must learn his secret. I demand you take me to him at once."

Utnapishtim took a deep breath.

"You have found him, son," he said. "I am the person you seek. I am Utnapishtim the Faraway."

Gilgamesh stared at the old man in disbelief. His knees buckled. He collapsed to the ground. His shoulders heaved up and down as he breathed heavily. He buried his face in his hands. And then, unable to arrest the gushing flood welling up in his eyes, he wept bitter tears.

Chapter 3: The Meal

Compassion stirred in Utnapishtim's heart. He felt sorry for the young man. He wanted to console him, but how? He needed help. It was obvious Urshanabi would be of no use. I wish Wife were here, he thought. She would know how to handle this. He realized what he had to do.

"Come with me, son," he said, stepping closer to the young man. "Come, Gilgamesh. Let's go find Old Woman and see if she can give you something to eat. You look worn out. You'll feel better after you've had some food and drink in your belly. Come on. Get up. Let's go."

He put his hand on Gilgamesh's shoulder and prodded him to get on his feet. A deflated Gilgamesh stood up, head bowed, shoulders hunched. All arrogance and bluster had been sucked out of him. His large, dark eyes rested on Utnapishtim's face, conveying a look of bewildered resignation. He leaned on Utnapishtim's arm, allowing himself to be led like a child. The two trudged toward the cabin at a snail's pace with Utnapishtim leading the way and Gilgamesh a few steps behind, dragging his feet.

Utnapishtim glanced behind him.

"Urshanabi, run on ahead and tell Old Woman to expect company. Ask her to prepare a nourishing meal for this young man."

"Yes, Master. Right away, Master."

Urshanabi lifted his dust-covered robe above his ankles and scampered off as fast as his legs could carry him on the soft, sinking sand. He was relieved to be of service. Maybe if I behave myself, Utnapishtim will forget his anger toward me for bringing a stranger to this faraway land, he thought. He made his way up to the house and found Old Woman waiting at the door. She had watched the encounter on the seashore and could see the men heading for the house.

"So, he's bringing the young man up here?" she asked, not waiting for Urshanabi to speak.

"Yes, Mother. And he wants you to prepare some food for him," Urshanabi panted, trying to catch his breath.

"I thought as much."

She grunted as she made her way to the kitchen. Urshanabi waited, expecting her to shower him with a series of questions. But the old woman said nothing. Instead, she began scuttling about in the kitchen. She brought out her containers and utensils, threw in some meat and vegetables to make a stew, set the fish to fry, and put some fresh bread to warm near the fire. Her fingers moved deftly, a movement that came with decades of knowing the way around her kitchen. By the time Utnapishtim and Gilgamesh had made their way to the front door, the savory aroma of cooked food saturated the house. Utnapishtim came through the door first.

"Wife," he called out to her. "Old Woman, where are you? I've brought a guest to break bread with us."

Old Woman emerged from the kitchen, wiping her hands on a dish cloth.

"This is Gilgamesh," he said, introducing his guest. "He is King of Uruk. He says he's part man, part god."

It was a perfunctory introduction, but it was all he was inclined to offer. He plopped down on a nearby chair and waited, satisfied he had performed his duty. Old Woman greeted this part man, part god with a token nod of her head. She retreated to the kitchen to finish preparing the meal.

Within a few minutes, the old man's head started bobbing up and down. He had dozed off in his chair, his breathing heavy and clearly audible. Urshanabi crouched in the corner, not knowing whether to stand or sit. After a cursory glance at his surroundings, the young man slouched on a nearby wooden chair and buried his face in his hands. He rocked his body backward and forward. Old Woman stole an anxious glance at him out of the corner of her eye. She had been through much in her lifetime and recognized the signs of distress. She bustled about in the kitchen, and before too long, the meal was ready. She placed the steaming hot food of stewed meat, vegetables, fried fish, and freshly warmed bread on the table. She laid three plates and called out.

"Husband, food is ready." No response.

She called out again, louder this time. "Utnapishtim, wake up! Food is ready!"

Roused from his slumbers, Utnapishtim sat up with a jerk. "Huh . . . What?"

"I said food is ready."

Utnapishtim rubbed his eyes and looked around. He saw Urshanabi crouched in the corner and Gilgamesh slouched on the wooden chair.

"Come and eat, son," he invited Gilgamesh, making it a point to ignore Urshanabi. "You'll feel better after you've eaten. Come. Old Woman has cooked a nice meal for us."

Gilgamesh got up as if in a daze and made his way to the table. Old Woman scowled. She motioned to Utnapishtim and inclined her head toward Urshanabi. He knew what she wanted him to do, but he wasn't willing to do it. The woman motioned to him again, this time nodding with more force. She wore a determined expression on her face indicating she would brook no argument.

"Wife, you give me no peace," Utnapishtim mumbled under his breath. He raised his voice, "Urshanabi, come and break bread with us."

Urshanabi jumped up, leaping at the opportunity to make amends with his master. Breaking bread together was as good a beginning as any, he reasoned. Besides, he felt the pinch of hunger, and the aroma of food was inviting.

"Thank you, Master," he said, taking his seat opposite Gilgamesh.

The three men ate without speaking, while the woman hovered around the table, making sure to replenish each plate as soon as it had been emptied. She refilled each of their cups. She served them in silence and observed them in silence. They ignored her presence, focusing with intent on the meal set before them. The room was quiet except for the sounds of the chewing and crunching and grinding of teeth. Eventually, each man had had his fill. He pushed his plate away with a grunt to indicate he was done. In turn, each reclined in his chair and let out a sigh.

"Aaah! That was a good meal, Old Woman," Utnapishtim sighed.

"Yes, it was," Gilgamesh echoed to no one in particular. He looked up and was startled to see the woman in front of him, having just been made aware of her presence. He examined her closely. He observed the wrinkles lining her face and the thin wisps of white hair that had escaped from under her head scarf. But what struck him most were her eyes. They were almond-shaped and piercing, capable of penetrating right through his skin. He felt exposed and vulnerable. He averted her gaze and looked down at the floor, feeling awkward and uncomfortable. But when he lifted his eyes to look at her again, he saw the corners of her mouth turn up in a smile. He searched her eyes and thought he recognized a glimmer of kindness.

"Delicious, as always," Urshanabi added. "Thank you, Mother."

The woman did not respond but began clearing away the table.

"Now, son," Utnapishtim said. "Why don't you tell us your story?"

"What do you want to know?" Gilgamesh asked.

"Anything and everything. Begin at the beginning," Utnapishtim prompted him. "You are Gilgamesh, part man, part god. Who is your mother? Your father? Who is this Enkidu you speak of with such passion? How did he die?"

At the mention of Enkidu's name, Gilgamesh was swept up in a wave of sorrow. He buried his face in his hands and shook his head in despair.

"Enkidu, my friend, my brother . . . Enkidu . . . My Enkidu is dead," he said stifling a sob.

Utnapishtim turned to the old woman, a baffled expression on his face. He shrugged his shoulders. He had no idea how to comfort the young man. He raised his eyebrows, tilting his head toward the grieving man, his eyes pleading with her to intervene. Knowing her husband's limitations, Old Woman went up to Gilgamesh. She tapped him gently on his shoulder and offered him a cup of water. Gilgamesh drained the cup.

"Who is your mother, Gilgamesh?" she asked, speaking to him for the first time. Her voice was hoarse but her tone was soft and kind. "You'll feel better after you tell us your story, son."

"My mother is the goddess Ninsun. My father is King Lugalbanda." Gilgamesh spoke in a hushed voice, barely above a whisper. "I am Gilgamesh, King of Uruk."

"Yes, son. Go on."

Gilgamesh expected the announcement to generate some measure of respect. But Old Woman seemed unimpressed.

"I am King of Uruk," he repeated. "The city of Uruk belongs to me. All its citizens and their sons and daughters are my possessions," he boasted, gradually raising his voice. "I am king. I am strong. I don't need sleep. I have power over everything. Power over everyone in Uruk."

His bragging intensified. "I can do as I please," he said. His voice strengthened with each word he uttered. "I can snatch children away from their parents and make them mine. No one dares to oppose me. I have the right to take a young virgin for myself on the eve of her wedding night. And when I am done with her, I send her crawling back to her father or husband." By now his voice was strong as he strutted his words out with increasing swagger.

Urshanabi chuckled, nodding his head in appreciation. But he stifled his laugh as soon as he caught Old Woman glaring at him.

"Really?" Old Woman said, feigning surprise. "Tell me, son. Why would you do that? Why would you snatch a young girl from her mother or a bride from her husband?"

She shook her head. Here we go, again, she thought. Male bravado rearing its ugly head. She made no attempt to conceal the disapproval in her voice. She concluded the young man was just another fool. He will no doubt brag about his powers, think he can do what he wants, when he wants, with whomever he wants, and with no regard for the consequences. So irresponsible. And so very, very tiresome. She looked at him quizzically, trying to make up her mind whether to feel sorry for him or slap some sense into him.

"Huh? Why would I do that? Why? Because I am Gilgamesh, King of Uruk," he snapped.

"Get on with your story, son," she said. Her tone indicated she was unimpressed by his bluster.

"I was content. I could do anything I wanted. But my people were not happy. At least that's what mother told me. They complained about me to the gods, accused me of being a tyrant. I wasn't a tyrant. I didn't hurt them. I took only what was rightfully mine. But they complained anyway." Gilgamesh shrugged his shoulders.

"Well, can you blame them?" Old Woman said, arching her eyebrows, waiting for a response. "Why do you think they complained?"

Gilgamesh looked up at her, startled that anyone would dare to challenge him. He ignored her question.

"The gods heard their lament and together they went to Anu, the father of the gods. They pleaded with him to help the people of Uruk before their cries became overwhelming. So Anu called upon Aruru, the mother of creation. He told her to create a human that would be my double. He was to be equal to me in strength and courage. This was to be my brother, Enkidu."

Gilgamesh paused. His eyes pooled with tears upon remembering Enkidu.

"Enkidu was beautiful," he said, looking up at Old Woman, tears in his eyes. "He was powerful, brave, and fierce. Aruru fashioned him from clay and tossed him in the wilderness among the animals. He told me he knew nothing of the cities of men in those days. He was a wild man. His hair was matted and thick, growing down to his waist. He lived with animals. He ate and drank with gazelles, with antelopes, with deer. He roamed freely among them. He was one of them. They embraced him as one of their own. He was happy.

"But one day, while he was drinking alongside the animals at a waterhole, a trapper saw him. The trapper was frightened. He had never seen such a strong, wild-looking man. He looked half animal, half human. The trapper told his father. His father sent him to me. That's when I first heard of Enkidu."

He repeated the name Enkidu several times, more to himself than to his audience. And then he swallowed hard and fell silent, burying his face in his hands.

Old Woman and Utnapishtim exchanged glances. Utnapishtim inclined his head toward Gilgamesh as if encouraging her to console the young man. But she shook her head and shrugged her shoulders. When Utnapishtim opened his mouth to speak, she gestured to him to attract his attention. Be patient and keep silent, she said to him with her eyes.

Chapter 4: The Wild Man

She made them wait in silence. Men! What is it with them? she thought. They have such little patience. They have no understanding of grief. Don't they know certain things can't be hurried? She looked around the room. Urshanabi fidgeted in his chair, his eyes darting nervously around the room. And as for Utnapishtim—well, you would think by the expression on his face he was writhing in agony. He looked at her with eyes urging her to prompt the young man to continue with his story. She ignored him.

She knew grief. She knew from bitter experience the recounting of events riddled with pain could not be rushed. The young man had to be given the time and space to speak when he was ready. She stood by his side and waited, stroking him gently on the shoulder. After several minutes of strained silence, the young man looked up at her, his eyes searching her face for some sign of empathy. He found it. Old Woman recognized his gaze as an indication he was ready to continue.

"So, son," she said, prompting him. "Go on with your story. How did you and this Enkidu of yours meet?" She took the seat near him, smiling and nodding encouragingly.

"The trapper came to see me in Uruk," he began.

His voice had grown stronger. Maybe the meal had done him some good, she thought. Maybe he also felt relieved at being able to talk about his experience.

"He stood before me and described Enkidu," Gilgamesh continued. "He said he was the strongest man he had ever seen. He said Enkidu was like an animal. He lived among animals, ate and drank with them, and could out-run any of them. He was more animal than human. The trapper was upset because Enkidu was rescuing animals by freeing them from his traps. He asked for my help to stop Enkidu.

"I was curious to learn more about this man who lived like an animal, a man who had never experienced human civilization. What was this creature like? Was he so strong he could even defeat me, the strongest man in Uruk? I was anxious to meet him. I suspected once he had been initiated to the world of men, the animals would reject him. He would be forced to enter the society of humans. And so I told the trapper what he needed to do." Gilgamesh paused, taking a deep breath.

"And what was that?" Utnapishtim asked, impatient to move the story along.

"I followed our traditions of initiation," Gilgamesh said. "I reasoned Enkidu was like a child since he'd never been exposed to the city. He didn't know what it meant to behave as a grown man in a civilized society. I remembered our traditions. I instructed the trapper to follow the same traditions we keep when a young boy is old enough to make the change from boyhood to manhood."

Gilgamesh stopped speaking and searched their faces. He hesitated to say more, wondering if they knew anything about these traditions.

Old Woman knew where he was going with his story. Although she was old and had lived in isolation for many years, there was a time when it wasn't so. She knew all about the traditions of marking a young boy's progress into manhood. She was proud of those time-honored traditions. There were some things you don't forget. This was one of them.

"Go on with your story, son," she said. "We know about these traditions." She smiled encouragingly.

He looked at her, a curious expression on his face.

"I sent the trapper to the Temple of the goddess Ishtar," he continued. "I told him to ask for one of the

GILGAMESH OF URUK

sacred priestesses." He paused to examine their faces, again. He hesitated. "The sacred priestess pays homage to the goddess by offering her body to any man who seeks physical and spiritual union with the goddess," he offered by way of explanation.

Old Woman's expression indicated her frustration. He must think we're ignorant because we live out here, she thought. She wanted to knock him down, to tell him these traditions existed long before his time, long before he was even a seed in his mother's belly, to tell him she knew more about tradition than he ever would. But she resisted. Not now, she said to herself. Maybe later. She smiled.

"Go on with your story, son."

"I advised the trapper to ask specifically for Shamhat because I was accustomed to her. I knew she could handle the challenge well." He spoke with a flourish as if he had made a bold announcement, as if he were expecting his listeners to be shocked. His eyes swept their faces, his mouth sporting a mischievous grin.

No one was surprised by his advice. They were familiar with the Temple of Ishtar and knew all about the sexual services the sacred priestesses willingly provided to men in honor of the goddess. This was a time honored and well-respected tradition, one that had been practiced for many years—more years than he had been alive. The tradition reenacted the sacred marriage, the life force that throbs within all living things and propels them toward growth and regeneration. Boys became men through sexual union with the sacred priestess. And men, even old men, who sought the physical and spiritual blessings of the goddess, engaged in sexual intercourse with her priestess to reaffirm these blessings.

"Wait a minute," Old Woman said. "Aren't the sacred priestesses still housed in the Temple of Ishtar?"

she asked. "Don't they have to stay within her sacred precinct to be available to men who seek the goddess' blessings? Isn't that so? Or have things changed since our time?"

"No, they haven't changed," Gilgamesh replied. "Any man who wishes to commune with the goddess journeys to Ishtar's temple and seeks her sacred priestess."

"Then I don't understand," she said. "As a wild man, Enkidu was ignorant of our ways. He knew nothing of the Temple of Ishtar. He knew nothing of the sacred priestess or the role she plays in initiations. So how was the trapper able to convince him to go to the Temple of Ishtar?"

"He didn't convince him," Gilgamesh replied with a smirk. "Enkidu didn't go to the Temple of Ishtar."

"Huh? What do you mean, son? I don't understand. You're going to have to explain."

"It's quite simple." Gilgamesh grinned at her. "I bent the rules a little. I am king. I can do that. Instead of Enkidu going to the temple, I told the trapper to take the temple to Enkidu. I told him to take Shamhat with him to the wilderness to wait near the waterhole for Enkidu to show up. She would provide the services of the sacred priestess from there."

Old Woman was surprised.

"Well, I've never heard of that happening before." She leaned back in her chair to think it through. "I didn't know it was even possible. I didn't think the goddess Ishtar would sanction the removal of her sacred priestess from the temple to perform her duty."

"Neither did I," Utnapishtim said.

"Nor me," Urshanabi added, always anxious to contribute his voice to the discussion.

"It's more customary for the man to go to the temple rather than to take the priestess to the man," Gilgamesh said. "But Enkidu wasn't a typical man and these weren't typical circumstances. I knew Shamhat well enough to know she wouldn't hesitate to perform her duties no matter how unusual the circumstances. And, besides," he added, "I'm king so she had to do as I commanded. As for the goddess Ishtar . . . Well . . ." Gilgamesh hesitated. "I reasoned what she didn't know wouldn't hurt her."

"Go on, son. Tell us what happened." Old Woman was anxious to hear more about this unique approach. "Did the trapper do as you suggested? Did it work?"

"Yes, it worked. The trapper did exactly as I suggested," Gilgamesh said. "He spoke to Shamhat, and she agreed to do as he asked. It all went according to plan."

Gilgamesh leaned back in his chair, looking thoroughly pleased with himself at accomplishing the improbable. His grin went from ear to ear. He took a few minutes to savor the moment and collect his thoughts before continuing.

"After Enkidu and I became friends, I asked him about his initiation into manhood. He said on the day it happened, he had gone up to the waterhole as usual and knelt down to drink water. That was when he saw her. He didn't know what she was since he'd never seen a woman before. She lay naked before him, revealing her breasts and her thighs. She lay with her legs apart and touched her herself.

"Enkidu said he didn't know what to make of her. He approached her cautiously, sniffing the air around her. And then he got closer and sniffed her body. He liked the smell of her. The woman touched him on his thigh, stroked his man parts, and gradually guided his penis inside her. He was aroused. At first, he didn't know what was happening. She kissed him and allowed him to caress her body. He soon forgot everything. He said he was overcome with desire. Shamhat did her job well. She seduced him through her many feminine charms. I knew she was capable. I knew she wouldn't disappoint." Gilgamesh grinned. "Enkidu boasted he made love to her continuously for seven days in a row." He laughed at the memory of his friend bragging about his sexual prowess.

Urshanabi nodded his head and chuckled. He stopped himself abruptly and glanced at Old Woman nervously, uncertain of her reaction. He knew from past experience she harbored some strange beliefs about the role of women. He had heard her argue with Utnapishtim numerous times, criticizing unfair practices toward women. But on this occasion, Urshanabi was safe. Although some women had begun to resent the tradition and criticized the role of the sacred prostitute, Old Woman wasn't one of them. She bowed her head, the corners of her mouth turning up into a meek smile, remembering. Urshanabi relaxed and eased back into his chair.

She was old, but she wasn't so old that she couldn't remember the passions of youth. She stole a furtive glance at Utnapishtim. He had a glint in his eyes and returned her smile, as if he, too, recollected the many times they had been wrapped in each other's arms in a heated embrace. They sighed simultaneously, their eyes exchanging the same wistful expression.

"Such a long, long time ago," Utnapishtim mumbled, more to himself than to anyone in the room.

"What?" Gilgamesh said. "Did you say something? I didn't hear what you said."

"Nothing, son," Utnapishtim replied. "I didn't say anything. Go on with your story." He glanced at Old Woman. A gentle blush faded from her cheeks. They shared a smile. He, too, was remembering.

"After he had pleased himself with the woman, Enkidu got up to rejoin the animals," Gilgamesh resumed his tale. "But just as I'd suspected, they scattered when they saw him. They could smell the human in him. He was no longer one of them. He had become a man. He was now aware of things animals couldn't know. He tried to chase after them but he couldn't keep up. That's when he knew he'd lost his animal strength. He didn't know what to do or where he belonged. He was lost. He went back to Shamhat. He sat humbly at her feet, acknowledging her as his teacher and guide."

Gilgamesh looked around the room. He had their attention.

"Shamhat spoke to him and he found himself understanding the language of men. She explained he had changed because he'd been with a woman. He was now a man. He could no longer live in the wilderness among animals. She told him about the city, describing Uruk and its wonders. She described the magnificent Temple of Ishtar. And she told him about me, Gilgamesh, the King of Uruk. She told him I was the strongest and most powerful man alive. Enkidu said she also told him I was arrogant, that I oppressed my people." Gilgamesh fell silent. His brow knitted into a frown. He looked troubled.

Old Woman exchanged a knowing glance with Utnapishtim. They shared the same thought.

"Go on, son," she prompted him.

"Now that he was no longer a wild man of nature, Enkidu was excited to go to Uruk," Gilgamesh said. "Shamhat's description of the splendor and festivities of the city had aroused his interest." He paused. "Have you ever been to Uruk?" he asked, turning to Utnapishtim.

"No. But I've certainly heard of its wonders."

"It's a beautiful city," Gilgamesh bragged. "It is the most noble city on earth. It boasts a Temple to Ishtar unlike any other in beauty and size. The land is plush with orchards and palm trees. Waterfalls grace the gardens. The city bustles with commerce in shops, marketplaces, and the public square. The people dress in fine colorful linens and embroidered wools. The women are beautiful with their dark, flowing hair and kohl-lined eyes. Every day there's music, singing, and dancing in the streets. The city bursts with life and joy and celebration."

Gilgamesh closed his eyes, remembering his city, feeling the pangs of homesickness. Old Woman read his expression. She recognized the feeling, the yearning to be home in a familiar surrounding with family and friends. She let out a sigh.

Gilgamesh sat up with a jolt and opened his eyes.

"Shamhat described the wonders of Uruk to Enkidu. She promised to take him to the Temple of Ishtar. She promised to take him to see the other priestesses. All were ready to offer themselves sexually to any man in honor of the goddess.

"Enkidu was excited. He wanted to go right away. But more than anything else, he was eager to meet me. Now that animals were no longer his friends, he wanted to make a new friend. He was lonely. Like me. He wanted a friend, a brother. Like me. He bragged to Shamhat he would declare himself the mightiest of men. He would challenge me to a fight to prove himself worthy of my friendship.

"Shamhat was wise. She knew Enkidu was not yet ready for city life. He had to pace himself. She spoke softly to him. She told him I was taller and stronger than any man alive—even stronger than him. She said I was blessed with a powerful life-force. I was loved by the gods. They had endowed me with strength and wisdom."

Gilgamesh puffed out his chest, smiling broadly. He stopped speaking, searching the faces of his listeners for a reaction. But no one looked impressed. Disappointed, he lowered his eyes. It was the first time in his life he had met people who were unimpressed by his bluster. He looked bewildered, lost in his own thoughts until Utnapishtim jolted him back to reality.

"Get on with your story, son."

Chapter 5: The Sacred Prostitute

And then he surprised them.

"Enkidu told me she described my dream," he said.

"Dream? You had a dream?" Old Woman perked up in her chair. Dreams were her specialty. She had developed quite a reputation as a skilled interpreter of dreams in her community. But that was a long time ago. That was before the great calamity had swept all the people away, leaving only a handful of survivors.

"It was a dream I had just before Enkidu came into my life," Gilgamesh said.

"If it happened before Enkidu came into your life, how did Shamhat know about it?" she asked. "Did you tell her?"

"No, I didn't tell her. Come to think of it, I don't know how she knew," Gilgamesh said, a puzzled expression on his face. "The only person I told about my dream was my mother, the goddess Ninsun. I wanted her to interpret it for me. Maybe mother shared it with Shamhat." He hesitated. "I don't know," he repeated. "Maybe Shamhat has special powers or maybe she learned of it through the goddess Ishtar."

Quite possible, thought the old woman. She had heard the many rumors of Shamhat's unique relationship with the goddess Ishtar. Shamhat was known to be a favorite of the goddess. She had been granted special privileges and honors. It was certainly feasible for the goddess to endow her with knowledge denied to others. Yes, that's probably what happened, she decided.

"Tell us your dream." Old Woman's curiosity was piqued. "What was it about?"

"I dreamt I saw a bright, shining star shoot across the sky. It fell at my feet. I tried to lift it, but it was too heavy. I tried to push it, but it was too big. Like a huge boulder. The people of Uruk gathered around it. We stared at it. Then, somehow, it changed its shape. It turned into baby."

"A what?" Utnapishtim barked in frustration. It was obvious from the tone of his voice he had no interest in dreams or their meanings.

"A baby."

"Hmm." Old Woman leaned toward him. "A baby, you say? That's interesting."

New life? New beginnings? New happenings? The death of the old, the birth of the new. The different possibilities raced through her mind.

Gilgamesh looked at her expectantly, waiting for her to say something. But she wasn't ready. She wanted to hear more.

"Go on, son."

"The people stroked it. They kissed its feet. I lifted the baby in my arms. I embraced it. I took the infant to mother. I laid it before her. That's when I woke up. I remembered the dream. I described it to mother so she could tell me what it meant."

"And what did your mother say? How did she interpret it?"

"She said the dream foretold of the coming of a companion for me. She explained the boulder in my dream represented a strong hero. He would be a brother to me, my second self, my double. She told me he would be loyal to me. He would fight by my side against all dangers. She said I would love him the way a man loves his wife."

Gilgamesh paused. "She was right," he said. "I loved Enkidu. I loved him as a man loves his wife. I loved him even more than that. He was better than a wife. He was my companion. And now . . . now he's gone. He's no longer with me. My beloved Enkidu has left my side forever."

Gilgamesh bowed his head and stared at the floor. He wrung his hands in despair. He took several deep breaths, suppressing the urge to cry. He fidgeted in his chair, lost in his thoughts.

"Your mother is good at interpreting dreams." The old woman smiled, nodding her head approvingly. "In the old, old days, people used to come to me to interpret their dreams. But that was before . . . that was long before . . ." Her voice trailed off.

Utnapishtim fidgeted uncomfortably in his chair.

"Get on with your story, son," he said. He cast an anxious look in Old Woman's direction.

"Yes, of course," Gilgamesh said. He glanced curiously at the old woman and then at Utnapishtim before continuing with his story.

"Shamhat interpreted my dream to Enkidu. She told him he would fulfill the promise of my dream. He would become my close companion. But she knew he wasn't ready to be brought to Uruk just yet. He wouldn't know how to behave. He'd spent his entire life mingling with animals. Uruk is a civilized city filled with culture and tradition." Gilgamesh declared these words emphatically as if daring his listeners to contradict him.

"Enkidu would need help to adjust to its ways, to gain the acceptance of its people. So Shamhat insisted on teaching him the ways of men and the city before bringing him to Uruk. She clothed him in one of her robes. She led him to a shepherd's hut. Enkidu said he followed her. He was like an innocent child. He didn't know what was in store for him. He didn't know what to expect. But he trusted her, trusted she would show him the way.

"Shamhat taught him to drink what humans drink, to eat what humans eat. She guided him until he became more comfortable living with humans. He learned to sit alongside the shepherds at the table to eat his meals. He tasted bread. He drank beer for the first time in his life. He said he didn't like the taste of it at first. He scrunched up his face to show me how he felt after taking the first sip."

Gilgamesh smiled, remembering, reliving happier times.

"Enkidu told me it took him a while to get used to drinking beer," he said. "In the beginning, his face would turn red with just a few sips. He would slur his words, become giddy with excitement. But he soon learned to handle it. Just like a real man. He couldn't get enough of it. He was proud of himself. 'If this is what it means to be a man,' he told Shamhat, 'I am become a man.'"

Gilgamesh looked up at Old Woman, searching her eyes. She returned his smile, nodding encouragingly.

"Enkidu still looked like a wild man. So Shamhat even had to tame his appearance. She cut his hair. She bathed him. She rubbed soothing oils on his body. He was tall, strong, and beautiful. He was so beautiful. He was the most beautiful man I've ever seen. His muscles were taut; his black hair clustered around his face in curls."

Gilgamesh buried his face in his hands.

"Why did he die? I don't understand." He shook his head vigorously. "We did everything right. Why did he die?"

Old Woman gently stroked his back.

"Son, who knows what the gods have in store for us? Only they know. Finish your story. Maybe we can help you understand what happened," she prompted him.

Gilgamesh swallowed hard before continuing.

"Enkidu became a friend to the shepherds. He protected their flocks from animals while they slept. He became a civilized man. Shamhat had done well to strip him of his wild ways. She tamed him. She prepared him for his entry into civilization.

"He wanted to come to Uruk. But Shamhat still didn't think he was ready. And then something happened. One day he met a man on his way to attend a wedding at Uruk. The man was angry. He was the uncle of a bride. He said the bride was forced to wait in the marriage bed for me after the wedding ceremony. He said I insisted on being the first to enter every bride. It was only after I had taken her maidenhead that the husband would be permitted to enter her. The gods had decreed it that way."

Gilgamesh looked up at Old Woman.

"It's not my fault," he said. "Anyway, none of that has anything to do with what happened to Enkidu."

He squirmed in his chair uncomfortably. He wasn't used to explaining himself. He suspected she wouldn't approve. He was right.

"It was the gods who decreed I should take every bride's maidenhead," he repeated, fidgeting awkwardly. "I was just performing the will of the gods."

"How do you know that?" There was a sharp edge to her voice.

"How do I know what?"

"How do you know the gods decreed you should take the maidenhead of every virgin? Did any of the gods actually tell you that?"

"Well, no, not exactly," Gilgamesh said. He sensed the anger rising in her voice.

"Then how do you know? How can you be so sure? Maybe this is some feeble excuse to satisfy your lust at the expense of these innocent young girls."

"What do you mean? What are you saying?" His eyes flashed with anger. "Are you saying I didn't have the right? Are you forgetting who I am? I am king of Uruk! It's my right. I can do what I want. It was the gods . . . It was the gods who decreed I should take the maidenhead of every virgin."

He spoke haltingly, his words stumbling over each other.

"I am king. I can do what I want. They are my subjects. They belong to me."

Old Woman scoffed. Her face tensed with disapproval. It was just so typical, she thought. Things haven't changed that much since my time. They think women are there for the taking. They use and abuse them to satisfy their lust. When they're done with them, they toss them aside like rotted fruit. She shook her head in disgust.

Gilgamesh turned away from her with a curt dismissal. He looked to Utnapishtim and Urshanabi for support.

"You understand what I'm saying, don't you?" he asked.

But Utnapishtim and Urshanabi had more sense than to reply. They knew her opinions. Goodness knows they had heard them expressed many a time. They stared at Gilgamesh, their expressions blank and noncommittal. They had the good sense to keep quiet. They weren't going to say anything to set her off.

"I explained it to Enkidu after he and I became friends," Gilgamesh insisted. He didn't want to tussle with the Old Woman. But for the first time in his life, he wanted to explain himself, to defend his actions.

"Enkidu understood perfectly. But when he first heard the man speaking of my right to enter the bride, he became angry. He said he would go to Uruk and challenge me to a fight. He said he would declare himself stronger than me. He insisted. Shamhat finally agreed to bring him to Uruk. She felt he was ready. By now Enkidu had become a man. He had learned the ways of civilized men. They headed to Uruk. He led the way. Shamhat walked behind him."

"What?" Old Woman jerked in her seat. She wanted to be sure she had heard correctly. "What's that you say? Did you say Enkidu led the way and Shamhat walked behind him?"

"Yes." Gilgamesh looked puzzled. "What's wrong? What's the matter now?" he asked.

"Enkidu led and Shamhat had to walk behind him?"

Gilgamesh nodded. He looked at Utnapishtim, seeking his support.

"What's wrong with her?" he asked. "What did I say?"

Utnapishtim shrugged. He didn't want to get in the middle of it.

"Don't you think it's strange?" Old woman said. "Don't you think it's strange that Shamhat, the same Shamhat who taught Enkidu what it means to be a man. This same Shamhat, the sacred priestess who trained him on how to behave in a civilized society is expected to walk behind him when she'd been his teacher?" Her tone was heavy with disapproval.

"Strange?" Gilgamesh was surprised. "What do you mean, strange? No, it's not strange at all. Why would it be strange?"

"Well, wasn't it Shamhat who taught Enkidu how to be a man? If it weren't for her, Enkidu might still be running around in the wilderness like a wild animal. Isn't that so?"

"Yes. So, what? I don't understand what you're upset about," Gilgamesh said.

Old Woman tried to control the tremor in her voice. The boy had no sense of right or wrong, no decency. She was sure of that.

"Doesn't this woman deserve some credit?" she asked. "Remember, this was no ordinary woman. This was a priestess of the goddess Ishtar. How can you call yourself a king? A ruler of your people? Women make up half your people. Where would you be without women? And, yet, you don't treat them as equals. You don't even recognize their contribution."

"What do you mean? What are you getting at?"

Gilgamesh looked confused.

Urshanabi and Utnapishtim knew perfectly well what she meant. They had heard her on this subject many times before. Urshanabi sat very still, afraid to breathe, afraid to move, afraid to say anything. He had never understood her opinions or her rage at what she called the appalling treatment of women. She made no sense to him. The more she had tried to explain, the more he had backed away. He was thankful when she finally gave up trying to make him understand. After a few minutes of tense silence, he began fidgeting in his chair uncomfortably.

Utnapishtim rolled his eyes and sat back in his chair. He knew what was coming. Old Woman stared at him, scowling, her lips pursed. Stay out of this, she warned him with her eyes. Don't interfere. The boy has to be made to understand. Utnapishtim folded his arms and waited. He sighed.

Old Woman took a deep breath to control the tremor in her voice.

"What I'm saying is she was the teacher. He was the student. Shamhat taught him everything he needed to know. She transformed him into a civilized man. Doesn't that give her to right to walk alongside him, at least? Why should she have to walk behind him? I'm not suggesting she should walk ahead of him, just maybe alongside him. Don't you think it's strange that he who was the student feels he can lead while she who was the teacher is required to follow? Doesn't she deserve more respect? Why should she follow? Just because she's a woman?"

"Is that what you're upset about? Hah! Well, that's too bad," Gilgamesh replied, his tone haughty. He wore a bemused expression on his face.

"No, I don't think that's strange at all That's just the way things are. That's the way they've always been. Shamhat is a woman. She had a job to do. She did it. But now that Enkidu had become a civilized man, he has to be at the head. He's in charge. He leads the way. The woman has to follow. That's just the way it is in a civilized society. That's the way it will always be." Gilgamesh rounded his sentence with a flourish.

"In other words, now that she has done her job, Shamhat gets tossed aside as if she didn't matter? As if her contribution is worthless?"

"That's not what I meant," Gilgamesh said, his irritation mounting. "Of course, Shamhat matters. Without her, Enkidu would still be living in the wilderness, running around like a wild animal. But Shamhat is no fool. She knows her place in a civilized society. She knows that's just the way it is. She accepts it. She's a woman. She doesn't lead. Women can't lead. Shamhat does what all women do, what all women *should* do. She follows."

Old Woman's face turned red; her brow tensed into a frown; her eyes flashed with anger. In the long ago past, she had been known in her community for expressing some unusual ideas for her time. She had debated both men and women, had been outspoken about the unfair treatment of women, about women being denied the respect they deserved. Few people understood her. Fewer still agreed with her. Some women even argued with her. They insisted they were perfectly content with their lot as women. We know our place, they said, eyeing her with disdain. She had accused them of being foolish, of undervaluing their contributions, of allowing themselves to be used and tossed aside when society thought it no longer had any use for them.

She still had the fire in her, ready to let her words gush out in a torrent. But Utnapishtim interrupted her. He had held his tongue for as long as he could. He knew once she unleashed her opinions, there would be no stopping her.

"Never mind who walked ahead and who walked behind," he said gruffly. "Who cares if Shamhat led or if Shamhat followed? What difference does it make now?"

He gave Old Woman a stern look to silence her. It was a look that told her this was neither the time nor the place to prolong this argument. Deep down, she knew he was right. She swallowed hard. It made no difference now, anyway, she thought. None of it made any difference. She bowed her head in silence. Utnapishtim let out a sigh of relief.

"Gilgamesh," he said, turning to face him. "Finish your story about how you and Enkidu finally met."

"Yes, yes, of course," Gilgamesh nodded. He shrugged his shoulders.

Old Woman could tell he still didn't understand. He had taken women for granted all his life. He wasn't used to being challenged. Young women were probably bashful around him, speaking only when spoken to, answering in monosyllables. And older women were barely noticeable. She remembered how they used to shuffle down the streets under a mantle of invisibility. And here she was, an old woman with a voice. Unafraid to express opinions. Unafraid to challenge. He must think me very odd, she concluded, an amused expression on her face.

Chapter 6: The Fight

"Enkidu led and Shamhat followed all the way to Uruk," Gilgamesh repeated. He glared at Old Woman defiantly, challenging her to interject. He paused, waiting to see if she had any more to say on the subject. But she remained silent, her eyes lowered.

"Enkidu entered Uruk, swaggering down the main street. He was bold and full of confidence. The people of Uruk hadn't seen such confidence in anyone other than me. Crowds of people jostled to get a better view of him. They clustered around him. They stroked him. They touched his arms and legs. They gushed at his towering build and strength. Some even groveled at his feet and kissed them. It happened just as it had in my dream. Enkidu heard them whispering among themselves. They compared the two of us. Some claimed he could even match me in strength and skill. Their words only increased his appetite to meet me.

"Of course, I knew nothing of this until I got to the marriage house. The bride was waiting inside for me. She knew I was to have first right with her just as the gods had decreed."

Gilgamesh glanced at Old Woman, fully expecting her to interrupt him with a nasty comment or ask him another one of her annoying questions. She did neither. She merely scowled but remained silent. He pulled his gaze away from her and twisted around as far as he could to turn his back to her. He addressed his words to Utnapishtim.

"I got to the marriage house, ready and eager to claim my right, the right given to me by the gods," he said emphatically, nodding his head. "But I couldn't get inside because Enkidu blocked the entrance. He stood like a giant boulder at the door. He refused to let me inside. I was angry. I didn't know who he was or what he was. No one had ever dared to challenge me before.

"Get out of my way, I said.

"'I will not,' he challenged me. He folded his arms and straddled his legs. He dared to defy me. I could tell he was itching for a fight.

"Do you know who I am? I asked.

"'I know who you are. And I don't care,' he said.

"I tightened my fists. I was ready to throw a punch. 'I am Gilgamesh, King of Uruk,' I announced. I could feel my face heating up.

"'I know who you are. And I don't care,' he repeated."

Old Woman scoffed.

"I'd heard enough from this upstart stranger," Gilgamesh said, ignoring Old Woman. "I roared out my warrior cry. I rushed toward him. I grabbed him by the arms. He gripped mine. We fought. Uruk had never seen any fight like this. We grappled with each other. We pinned each other down. We struggled to get free. We staggered about. We flung each other on to doorposts and walls and houses. Our fight was fierce. It raged on. We careened down the streets of Uruk. The people lined the streets, watching and cheering. It was exhilarating. My heart pounded. I'd never known a man of such strength.

"We punched and pounded at each other. Blood streamed from our wounds. Our faces bruised and bloody. But neither was willing to surrender. We fought long. We fought hard. But I was the stronger of the two. I was finally able to force Enkidu to the ground. I held him there. I pinned down with my right knee. He couldn't escape.

"Our contest was over. I had won. Enkidu acknowledged my victory. He was gracious in defeat. He showered me with praise. He said my mother Ninsun had made me unique among humans by endowing me with such strength. He said the god Enlil was wise to give me the kingship of Uruk because I was the strongest of men. It was only right I should rule. My anger melted. I embraced him. He embraced me. Enkidu and I became brothers."

Gilgamesh paused, his head bowed, eyes lowered, mind awash with memories of happier times. He stifled a sob.

"We were friends. We were brothers. We swore loyalty to each other. We held hands. We walked down the streets of Uruk. The people lined the streets. They cheered us. They threw flowers at our feet. They were happy I had found a partner who was almost my equal in strength. Enkidu was my friend, my companion, my brother. I loved him as a man loves his wife. He never left my side. We were partners."

Gilgamesh's voice softened and trailed off.

"I took him to meet my mother Ninsun," he said. "She was happy I had found a partner, someone with whom I could share my life. But now . . ." Gilgamesh paused. He gulped, trying to hold back tears. "But now it's all over. Now my Enkidu is gone. He is gone forever."

He grew silent. He swallowed hard. His eyes pooled with tears.

"We used to do everything together," he said, his words punctuated by sobs. A wave of longing swept over him, seeping into his voice. "We played hard. We fought hard. We had mock fights to sharpen our skills and build our strength. We hunted together, ate together, drank together, slept together. We visited the Temple of Ishtar together. We were always together. He was my brother and my companion. If only . . . if only that had been enough. If only I had been satisfied with that."

Gilgamesh stumbled over his words. "If only Shamash hadn't given me such a restless spirit."

Gilgamesh lowered his eyes and stared at his sandals.

"What do you mean, son?" Utnapishtim asked. "What happened?"

Gilgamesh hesitated before replying.

"It's not my fault," he began. "Shamash had given me a restless spirit. Mother told me Shamash is to blame for the way I am."

Old Woman and Utnapishtim exchanged glances. The same thought occurred to both. Utnapishtim sighed.

Old Woman was the first to speak.

"What do you mean, son? Why are you blaming Shamash? What did he do to you?"

"I can't help myself. I'm restless. I get bored very easily. I can never settle down. I'm always wanting to try new things, go on new adventures. It's not my fault," Gilgamesh explained.

"Son, what did you do?" Old Woman asked.

Gilgamesh buried his face in hands. He didn't reply.

"Son, you're restless. There's nothing wrong with that," Utnapishtim said. "You're young. Of course, you want to try new things. That's very normal for a man your age. No one would expect you to be any different."

"Yes, but this was different," Gilgamesh replied, looking up at Utnapishtim. "After the novelty of having Enkidu as my partner had worn off, I got bored with the same old routine. I needed more of a challenge. I yearned for the thrill of an adventure. I wanted to do something exciting. I wanted to establish my name forever as a king, as someone who would be remembered for exceptional bravery and strength."

Gilgamesh took a deep breath. His listeners waited in anxious silence. An air of tension filled the room. Gilgamesh took another deep breath and resumed his tale.

"I don't know," he hesitated. "Maybe it was my fault, after all. Maybe it was all my fault."

He choked back tears. "Maybe I should never have suggested it. But I hungered for something exciting, something memorable. I wanted to be famous even beyond the walls of Uruk. I wanted to be remembered for all time. He tried to talk me out of it. Enkidu warned me, but I was too eager to go. If only I had listened to him. Perhaps he would still be alive today," he said, his hands shaking.

"What happened?" Utnapishtim asked, his voice showing a combination of concern and impatience. "What did you do, son? Out with it!"

Gilgamesh swallowed hard. "I decided to go to the Cedar Forest and kill the evil guardian of the forest, Humbaba. I wanted to rid the world of his evil."

He strung the words out in a rush. He lowered his eyes, unwilling to see the expression on the faces of his listeners.

His announcement was followed by a stunned silence. Old Woman was the first to speak. Her voice was hoarse.

"You did what? Why? What for? Had Humbaba caused you any harm?" she asked. "What evil had he committed against you?"

Gilgamesh looked up at her, his eyes pleading for understanding.

"Well, he didn't exactly do anything to us. But he was evil through and through. I just thought . . . well, I just thought the world would be a better place if we got rid of him," he whispered. He sounded apologetic, lowering his eyes again to avoid meeting her glare.

Old Woman raised her eyebrows in disbelief. Her brow tensed as she fixed her eyes on Gilgamesh.

"You mean to say . . . you mean to say you deliberately went out there to kill him even though he had done nothing to hurt you or your people?"

Gilgamesh nodded.

"But why? Why did you . . .? Didn't you know Humbaba was put there by the gods to protect the Cedar Forest? Why would you go after him? Why . . .?" The words came out haltingly as she searched for the right words to express her indignation. But she wasn't allowed to finish her sentence. Utnapishtim interrupted her.

"Let the boy finish his story," he said gruffly. His voice was stern enough to silence her.

Old Woman scowled. She wanted to speak her mind, to tell Gilgamesh what she thought of his foolhardy quest. But she held back.

"Enkidu tried to talk me out of it," Gilgamesh continued, raising his head to look at Utnapishtim. "He already knew the Cedar Forest from the days when he roamed freely among the deer and antelope. He said he was afraid to go back there. He said it was dark and deep and frightening and seemed to go on forever. He reminded me Humbaba was a fierce monster. The god Enlil had placed him to guard the Cedar Forest to prevent anyone from entering. I knew all about that. But it didn't stop me. I still wanted to go. I was desperate. I yearned for excitement, for another adventure. I wanted to cut down the huge cedar trees to build a big wall around the city of Uruk. I wanted people to remember me for my heroism. I wanted to be famous for all time." Gilgamesh's words tumbled out in rapid succession, one after the other.

"I have heard of this monster Humbaba," Utnapishtim said. "He terrified men. He breathed fire. He could crunch a man with his fierce jaws. Men trembled at the sound of his thundering voice."

"I've heard of him, too," Urshanabi added, eager to say something. He felt he had been silent for too long. "I'm surprised you wanted to face him when he hadn't done you any harm. All the stories about him describe him as a fierce monster. He could rip apart anyone who dared to enter the forest."

"Yes, that's what Enkidu told me. You sound just like him," Gilgamesh said looking at Urshanabi. "He tried to warn me. I ignored him." Gilgamesh paused, reflecting.

"Enkidu was scared, but I convinced him to go with me. I urged him to find his courage. Humbaba was an evil monster. We had to get rid of him, I said. I reasoned since we're all doomed to die anyway, why not die while on this great adventure? If I were to die in the forest fighting against Humbaba, people would say of me I had met a hero's death. What would they say of him if he failed to accompany me? I shamed him into believing people would say he was a coward. I'd made up my mind to kill Humbaba. I wanted those cedar trees. And I was going to do it with or without Enkidu. Either way, I would be famous. People would celebrate my bravery long after I was gone."

Gilgamesh lowered his eyes to avert the stares of his listeners. He squirmed, fidgeting awkwardly in his chair.

"I called out to the people of Uruk," he said, his voice subdued. "I wanted their support to convince Enkidu to go with me. They spilled out into the streets when they heard me. I declared my intention. I wanted my name to live forever. I turned to the young friends and warriors who had fought by my side in battle. I asked for their blessing so I could return victorious in time to celebrate the New Year with them.

"Enkidu did everything he could to prevent me from going. He stood up and spoke to the crowd. He wept. He pleaded with the elders of Uruk to stop me. He begged them to convince me to abandon my journey to the Cedar Forest. He repeated what he knew of Humbaba—that the fierce monster had the protection of the god Enlil and a challenge to him would offend the god who put him there."

"And yet you still insisted on going," Old Woman interrupted him.

Ignoring her interruption, Gilgamesh continued.

"Enkidu convinced the elders to agree with him. But I refused to give up. The elders tried to dissuade me. They accused me of being young and foolish. They said I was restless. They claimed no one could defeat Humbaba. But I didn't care. I paid no attention to them. What do they know? I just laughed them off. I was more determined than ever to go. I longed for adventure. I wanted to prove them all wrong. I wanted to show them I was unafraid." Gilgamesh took a deep breath and paused.

Old Woman looked at Utnapishtim and shook her head. He understood her alarm. He nodded slowly in agreement. They knew nothing good could come from deliberately hunting down a guardian performing the duty assigned to him by a god. Only a fool would seek trouble and provoke the gods. They had witnessed first-hand the wrath of the gods, and what they had witnessed would strike fear in the bravest of men.

"Go on with your story, son," Utnapishtim sighed.

"I taunted Enkidu in front of the crowd," Gilgamesh said, unaware of the concern he had generated with two of his listeners. "I asked him if he had the courage to go with me. I asked if he was still afraid of dying a hero's death. I said all this to him in front of everyone. I wanted to shame him. I left him no choice. The people would have accused him of being a coward if he had turned me down. Enkidu could only nod his head.

"We held hands. We embraced. We pledged our loyalty to each other again. We went to the smith to tell him what weapons we needed. I had silenced Enkidu's objections."

Gilgamesh hesitated. Speaking barely above a whisper, his throat dry, he said, "At the time, I didn't know the heavy price I would pay for getting what I wanted. If I'd only known . . ." He paused and looked down on his feet, stifling a sob.

Old Woman couldn't help but feel sorry for him. Yes, he had made a lot of foolish decisions. Yes, he was arrogant. But he was a child in a man's body. She stood up and handed him a cup of wine. He gulped it down. He took another deep breath before resuming his story.

"The smiths built us heavy weapons and armor, so heavy only men of exceptional strength could lift them," he said. "They made us axes each weighing two hundred pounds. They made us knives sheathed in mountings of solid gold. When all was ready, we went to my mother Ninsun. I wanted her blessing before we left."

Gilgamesh fell silent, burying his face in his hands.

Chapter 7: The Journey

Several minutes of a prolonged silence followed in which Urshanabi squirmed in his chair. Utnapishtim folded his arms, leaning back in his chair. Old Woman studiously examined Gilgamesh's face to see if she could read genuine remorse.

Gilgamesh resumed his story.

"We went to Ninsun's temple. I bowed before my mother. I told her my plan to go to the Cedar Forest, to take a journey no man had yet undertaken, to fight an enemy no man had yet defeated. I asked for her blessing to return victorious. I thought she would be proud of me. Instead, she was sad."

"Well, what did you expect, son?" Old Woman asked. She shook her head in wonder at the boy's naiveté. "She's your mother. She loves you. She's concerned about you. She doesn't want you to get hurt. And here you are telling her you plan to go on a dangerous mission, one that has no justification other than to quench your thirst for fame and glory. How do you expect a mother to react, especially when she knows her son plans to defy the god Enlil through his actions?"

"I expected her to be happy for me and support my decision," Gilgamesh snapped. The old woman with her intrusive comments and questions irritated him and he didn't hesitate to show it.

"Did she try to stop you, son?" Old Woman asked. "That's what I would have done had I been your mother."

"Well, you're not my mother," Gilgamesh retorted. "And, no, she didn't try to stop me. She knew I couldn't help myself. I told you before. Mother knew it was Shamash who was responsible for my restless spirit, for my hunger for adventure. It wasn't my fault."

"What did she say when you told her?"

"She went to her chambers. She told Enkidu and I to wait for her return. She soon came out wearing her finest robe and jewels. She beckoned me to join her. I followed her to the roof while Enkidu waited below. I watched and listened in silence as she lit incense and offered a prayer to the sun god Shamash.

"She reminded Shamash he had granted me beauty and strength. But he had also plagued me with the restless heart. She said it was my restless heart that was driving me to go on this dangerous journey. She blamed Shamash for the way I am." Gilgamesh cast a piercing look at the old woman as he spoke.

"She asked him to extend the daylight hours and to shorten the nights to help me," he continued. "She asked his bride, the goddess Aya, to entrust the stars to watch over me at night. And then she asked Shamash's help in subduing Humbaba. I remember her words very clearly. I remember them because I reminded Shamash of her prayer when Enkidu and I were in the Cedar Forest.

"'Stir strong winds—hurricanes and tornadoes—to pin Humbaba down,' she prayed to Shamash. 'Paralyze his movements. Let my Gilgamesh subdue him. Protect him. Protect my son. Let him come home to me victorious.'

"After mother and I came down from the roof, mother spoke to Enkidu. She adopted him as her son. She told him to be my brother, to guide me to the forest, to protect me, to bring me home victorious. She hung a jeweled amulet around Enkidu's neck. 'This is a token of my commitment,' she said to him. Enkidu was deeply moved. Tears filled his eyes. He clasped my hand as she spoke.

"After receiving mother's blessing, Enkidu and I carried our weapons. We made our way out of the city. The people of Uruk lined the streets to set us off on our adventure. They cheered and clapped for us. The musicians played their instruments. The girls danced in front of us as we walked. The atmosphere was festive and exciting. The whole city came out to see us off. They supported me. They wanted me to go on this journey."

Gilgamesh paused long enough to glare at the old woman.

"The elders silenced the crowds so their parting words of advice could be heard. They cautioned us to be careful. They entrusted Enkidu with my protection. They told him to walk ahead of me since he knew the way. They asked him to bring me back victorious. Then they coached us on what to do to be successful. They said we should dig a well each night to fill our water skins with fresh water in preparation for the journey the next day. They reminded us to make an offering to Shamash every evening to win his favor.

"The elders told me to remember my father, Lugalbanda. He, too, had journeyed to a far-off place and come back victorious. And, finally, they reminded Enkidu to fight by my side, to shield me from harm.

"I was excited and eager to set off on this new adventure. I wanted to walk in my father's footsteps. I wanted to come back victorious just as he had done. Enkidu didn't share my enthusiasm, but he never abandoned me. He was my brother. He said to me, 'Since you're determined to go on this journey, I have no choice but to accompany you. Come. Let us set aside all fear. Let us begin our journey. I'll walk before you. I'll lead the way since I know how to get to the Cedar Forest and Humbaba.'

"We set off. Enkidu led the way and I followed. We walked for four hundred miles before stopping to eat. And then we walked for another six hundred miles before stopping to pitch our tent for the night. We did as the elders had advised. Before the sun went down for the night, we dug a well. We filled our water skins to prepare for our journey the following day. And then I took some flour to the mountaintop and scattered it about as an offering to Shamash. I asked for a favorable dream. Meanwhile, Enkidu performed the ritual for dreams and asked for a sign. He built a shelter for the night. I lay on the floor while he spread a magic circle of flour around me for my protection. Enkidu slept across the doorway of the tent to shield me from any harm.

"I soon fell asleep. But I woke up at midnight, trembling with fear because of a horrible dream. My skin was crawling. I couldn't stop shivering."

Gilgamesh faltered in his speech, remembering the feelings of terror he experienced from his dream. He shuddered as a cold chill ran down his spine.

His listeners, wrapped in silence, listened intently to Gilgamesh's story. But at the mention of a dream, Old Woman spoke up.

"What was your dream about?" she asked, her curiosity piqued at the mention of another dream.

"It was strange. Enkidu and I were walking in a canyon. A huge mountain towered over us. It leaned heavily toward us. It kept leaning and leaning until it began to topple on top of us. We ran as fast as we could to get out of the way. But we weren't quick enough. The mountain crashed down on top of us, burying us. I couldn't breathe. I woke up in a cold sweat, petrified. I was so scared. I called out to Enkidu. He explained my dream. He said it was a favorable omen. Humbaba was the huge mountain. Like the mountain in my dream, Humbaba will crumble in defeat. Enkidu assured me the dream meant the god Shamash was on my side. He would grant us victory to overcome and kill Humbaba. I was comforted by his words. I was confident we would succeed."

Old Woman arched her eyebrows. She cast a skeptical look at Utnapishtim, shaking her head. He put his fingers to his lips, directing her to keep silent.

"The next day, we resumed our journey," Gilgamesh said. "We repeated the same routine: traveling for four hundred miles; stopping to eat; walking for another six hundred miles; digging a well and filling our water skins; pitching a tent; making an offering at the top of the mountain; and requesting a favorable dream. Enkidu performed the ritual for dreams. We slept. And I experienced another dream. But this time my dream was more frightening than the first."

Old Woman leaned forward attentively.

"There was a huge mountain. It grabbed me. It threw me to the ground. I tried to fight to get away. I struggled. But it held me too tightly. I couldn't move. My feet were pinned down. I couldn't get away. And then I couldn't see anymore. A blinding light hit my eyes. I struggled. I was frantic. I couldn't see. Then, out of nowhere, a man appeared. He came toward me. He was handsome. He was beautiful. His body gave off light. He sparkled as he moved. He pulled me from under the mountain. He cradled my head. He gave me water. I woke up.

"I was scared. I thought it was a bad omen. I shook Enkidu awake and asked him to interpret it for me. He listened to my dream. He assured me it was favorable. He said the mountain was Humbaba who tried to kill me but couldn't. The man giving off light who rescued me was none other than the god Shamash. 'The Lord Shamash will protect you and grant you victory,' Enkidu insisted. Once again, I was relieved."

"This Enkidu was quick to interpret dreams," Old Woman said, her tone dismissive. "How do you know he interpreted correctly?" she asked. "Who taught him this skill?"

"I don't know," Gilgamesh replied, irked at the ease with which she interrogated him. "Perhaps he taught himself when he was out in the wilderness among the animals. He seemed to have a natural skill at interpreting."

"Well, I'm not sure how natural or how good his skill was," Old Woman said, her tone skeptical. "But he certainly seemed to have convinced you of his know-how at dream interpretation."

Gilgamesh whipped his head around to face her. He cast a blistering look in her direction, hoping to silence her. His patience was wearing thin with her meddling comments and probing questions. She had no right to doubt Enkidu's skill. He wanted to leap in defense of his friend. Utnapishtim, sensing the potential for a clash, intercepted him and ended the exchange.

"Get on with your story, son." He glared at the woman. He had little interest in dreams or in a description of the long, drawn out journey to the Cedar Forest. Although he didn't approve of the whole escapade, he was still eager to get to the exciting part, to hear about the confrontation between Gilgamesh and Humbaba.

Gilgamesh refused to be hurried in his narrative. He found the old woman's questions and comments annoying, but he shared with her an interest in dreams. He refused to gloss over the telling of them since they formed an essential part of his story. Dreams illustrated for all to see the close bond he and Enkidu had enjoyed.

"We resumed our long journey on the third day," Gilgamesh continued. "We repeated the same routine, and that night, I had another dream."

Utnapishtim sighed in frustration. He folded his arms and leaned back in his chair with the look of a martyr waiting for the inevitable to happen. Urshanabi followed his lead and also heaved a weary sigh. Old Woman glared at them both. Her eyes darted from one to the other, cautioning them to keep their displeasure to themselves. She need not have concerned herself because Gilgamesh blithely ignored their disgruntled gestures.

"This time it was the heavens and earth. They were angry. The earth shaking with rage, the skies thundering fiercely. It was pitch black everywhere. Suddenly, lightning. Flashes of lightning struck the trees. They burst into flames. The fire was fierce, unyielding, scorching the earth. It covered everything with ash. It moved so quickly. I could feel the intense heat. It was coming right toward me. I tried to run away. I couldn't move my feet. I was stuck. It got hotter and hotter, closer and closer.

"I woke up, shaking and trembling all over. I woke Enkidu and asked him to interpret my dream. Once again, he reassured me. He said the anger in the heavens represented Humbaba who would try to kill me with flames, but he wouldn't prevail. 'We will defeat him and kill him,' Enkidu insisted. Enkidu was so good at interpreting dreams and making me feel better."

Out of the corner of his eye, Utnapishtim could see Old Woman cradling her chin and shaking her head. He thought she would interject another one of her snide remarks, but she remained silent, her eyes lowered. He sighed with relief.

"On the fourth day, we traveled as we had done on the three previous days and followed the same pattern. But that night my dream was the worst ever—more frightening than any of the others."

Old Woman glanced at Utnapishtim. He didn't say anything, merely rolling his eyes in frustration. But he was wise enough not to open his mouth to voice his objection, especially when it came to the topic of dreams. Years of living with her had taught him it was better not to challenge her on certain subjects, one of which was the value of dreams and her ability to interpret them.

"I saw a fierce eagle wearing a lion's head and shooting flames from its mouth. It floated down from the skies toward me," Gilgamesh continued, oblivious to the interplay of furtive glances and rolling eyes that were being exchanged in front of him. "The creature came straight for me. It screeched and squawked. I saw its eyeballs, red and angry. I tried to run. I couldn't move. My feet rooted to the ground. From nowhere, another young man appeared. Surrounded by light. He grabbed the creature before it could hurt me. He snapped its neck and wings. I heard the crunch of broken bones. The man flung it to the ground where it lay, dead. I saw its lifeless body on the ground.

"I woke Enkidu. Another good omen, he told me. 'The eagle was Humbaba who wants to attack you, but the god Shamash comes to your rescue again. He won't let Humbaba hurt you,' he assured me. I thanked him. I embraced him. Enkidu was my brother."

Gilgamesh paused. Looking up at the old woman, he baited her, "Enkidu was so clever at interpreting dreams. He always knew just what to say to make me feel better," he repeated.

Old Woman refused to take the bait. She stared into the distance. She waited.

"On day five, I dreamt I was in a fierce battle with a huge bull. We wrestled. The bull was big and powerful. I fought for my life. The bull pulled me down. It crushed me by its weight. I struggled. I tried to get out from under it. I could feel its panting breath on my face. I could smell it. It stank. I thought I was going to die. A young man emerged before me. Rescued me. Pulled me away from underneath the heavy weight. Revived me. Gave me fresh water. I woke up.

"'The bull is Humbaba,' Enkidu said. 'And this time the young man who rescues you is not Shamash. It is none other than your personal god and father, Lugalbanda.'"

"Lugalbanda?" Old Woman interrupted him. "Did you say, Lugalbanda?"

"Yes," Gilgamesh said, scowling. "Lugalbanda, my personal god and father." His tone was emphatic and curt, hoping to communicate his anger at her intrusions. More than anything else, he wanted to stop her incessant prying. It didn't work.

"And how did Enkidu know this was Lugalbanda when all the other times he said the young man was Shamash?" she asked, unfazed by his displeasure.

"I don't know," Gilgamesh snapped. "He told me it was Lugalbanda, and I believed him. I told you. Enkidu was skilled in interpreting dreams. Now . . . can I get on with my story?"

"Yes, son. Go on with your story," Utnapishtim said. He darted a menacing look at Old Woman. She shot a fierce look back at him, but she said nothing.

"Enkidu said Lugalbanda would help me defeat Humbaba. He told me I would achieve a greater triumph than any other man. He said my name would live forever."

Gilgamesh paused to take a deep breath. He had stressed the name Lugalbanda each time to irritate the woman. Since she didn't interject with another of her probing questions, he felt triumphant.

"By this time, we had arrived at the edge of the Cedar Forest. As we approached, I could hear Humbaba's hideous roar in the distance. The sound of his voice was frightening. I could feel my body shaking from head to foot. I could feel tears streaming down my face. I was afraid Enkidu and I would not be able to defeat such a fierce monster on our own. I remembered mother's prayer. I reached out to Shamash, asking him to protect me.

"Enkidu and I stood motionless, our feet frozen to the ground. We heard a voice call out from the heavens. It was the god Shamash. He encouraged us to move forward. The voice said, 'Gilgamesh, subdue Humbaba now before he has time to hide deep in the forest, before he drapes himself in the paralyzing glare of his seven auras. Attack quickly. Humbaba has draped himself in only one of his auras. He is at his weakest now. Don't delay. Go quickly.'

"Enkidu and I stood at the edge of the forest, staring into its darkness. It was dense with foliage. Humbaba could be hiding anywhere, ready to pounce on us should we dare to cross its threshold. We hesitated. We looked at each other, wondering the same thing. Should we or shouldn't we enter?"

Chapter 8: The Monster

She sensed their excitement. She saw it in their eyes. The young man certainly had captured their attention. Utnapishtim perked up, no doubt relieved at long last to get to the exciting part. She suspected he had been bored to tears by the dreams. He just didn't understand their importance. Called them nonsensical babble. She saw him lean forward in anticipation. Urshanabi followed his lead and did the same. It was so typical of them, she thought. They were eager to hear about raging battles and blood and gore and dismembered body parts. She shook her head, frowning in disgust.

Gilgamesh took a deep breath, sensing the air of anticipation in the room.

"Enkidu and I stared into the forest," he said. "We were awestruck by the amazing height and grandeur of the trees. They were so thick and tall. We could barely see the Cedar Mountain in the distance where the gods lived, a mountain sacred to the goddess Ishtar. It was magnificent with its slopes blanketed by cedar trees. The trees all around us exhaled a sweet fragrance. They shaded us from the scorching sun. The sights and scents were overpowering and inviting. I couldn't wait to cut the trees down and take them back to Uruk to show my people.

"Clearly visible in front of us was Humbaba's well-trodden path. Enkidu and I exchanged looks. We didn't have to speak. We knew what we had to do. We picked up our axes, unsheathed our knives, and entered the forest. We made our way along Humbaba's path.

"Enkidu walked ahead of me. We were cutting our way through thorns and shrubbery when Enkidu suddenly stopped dead in his tracks.

"'What is it my friend?' I asked. 'What's wrong?' His face had turned white and his body trembled.

"'I can sense his presence,' he said, a tremor in his voice. 'I can sniff him. He's nearby.'

"Enkidu spoke in a heavy whisper. I could barely hear him. I became anxious. Why was he whispering? I shuddered. Is Humbaba so close? Can he hear us? Is he watching us? Is he concealed behind the dense foliage? I stopped and listened for the sound of movement. But all was quiet except for the pounding of my heart. Not even the sound of a twig snapping or a leaf rustling in the wind broke the silence. I wiped the sweat trickling from my brow and stood, motionless.

"After a few minutes, Enkidu spoke again.

"'I can't go on,' he whispered. 'I'm too scared. Go on by yourself, Gilgamesh,' he urged me. 'Kill Humbaba. Cut down the trees without me. I'll go back to Uruk. I'll tell the people of your bravery. I'll tell the people I was a coward. I no longer care what they think of me. I'm too frightened to go any further. Please, Gilgamesh. Please let me go back.'

"'Enkidu, you can't leave me,' I pleaded. 'Think of how far we've come. I can't kill Humbaba on my own. You're my brother. You promised my mother. You promised the people of Uruk. You must stay and protect me. Don't be afraid. Together we'll be strong. Together we can defeat Humbaba.'

"'You don't know him,' Enkidu said, his voice full of dread. 'You don't know how fierce he is. You haven't seen him. I have. I know what he's like. He's terrifying. His teeth are like tusks and as sharp as knives. He has the face of a lion and the strength of a bull. He comes charging at you quicker than a bolt of lightning. His forehead shoots flames. His face is smeared with the blood of his victims. I'm terrified of him. I can't go on. Go ahead without me.'

"Enkidu, I can't go alone, I pleaded. By now sweat was pouring down my brow. I could see fear in Enkidu's eyes. I could taste fear on my tongue. But I refused to give up."

"Why, son?" Old Woman interrupted. "Why didn't you just turn around and go back with Enkidu? Why was this so important to you?"

"I've explained it to you already," Gilgamesh snapped. "I told you Shamash had made me restless. I wanted my name to live forever. I wanted the people of Uruk to remember Gilgamesh, their king. I wanted cedar trees to build the city wall. I wanted to protect the city from invaders. I wanted . . ."

"Yes, but son . . ."

"Go on with your story," Utnapishtim said, frowning at her.

Old Woman arched her eyebrows. She shook her head but said nothing. There was no point to it.

"I reminded Enkidu of his bravery in the past, running with wild animals, killing lions and wolves," Gilgamesh said, looking at the woman out of the corner of his eye. "I reminded him he had been tested in battle, that he was strong, that we were brothers, and that together we could defeat Humbaba."

Gilgamesh stopped speaking and looked down at his sandals to avoid seeing the faces of his listeners.

"The truth is . . . the truth is," he said finally, stumbling over his words and looking up at Old Woman. "I only half believed what I said to Enkidu. From everything I'd heard about Humbaba, I wasn't sure even the two of us working together would be a match for him. But I knew I couldn't go on without Enkidu. Humbaba would kill me for sure if I faced him alone.

"I was scared. But then I thought how could I face my people if I returned empty-handed? They would call me a coward. They would laugh at me. My name would forever be remembered as the king who went on a long journey and came back with nothing to show for it. I would be the king who was too afraid to face Humbaba. I couldn't survive the shame. I had to move forward even if it meant my death. I had no choice. I continued to plead with Enkidu until he agreed to fight Humbaba with me.

"Together we trudged deeper and deeper into the forest until we were standing in front of Humbaba's den. We froze. Humbaba must have seen us from inside his den. We heard him before we saw him. His voice boomed, making my blood run cold. I could feel his eyes fasten on me.

"'Prepare to die, you pathetic fools' he roared. 'You will never make it home alive.' His voice thundered across the skies.

"I was paralyzed with dread. My body shook. My teeth rattled. My heart pounded. I was tempted to turn back and run. But Enkidu gave me courage.

"'Don't be afraid,' he consoled me. 'Remember the boasts you made in Uruk. Now is the time to press forward and attack. You were right. You've nothing to fear. I'm by your side. It's just as you said. Together we can defeat Humbaba.'

"We moved cautiously toward the monster's den, ready to strike at a moment's notice. I signaled to Enkidu to approach from one side of the monster's den while I approached from the other. I thought by entering his den from opposite sides, we might confuse the monster long enough for one of us to thrust a knife into his body. But Humbaba had different ideas. He didn't wait for us to get close. He emerged from his den like a raging bull."

Gilgamesh took a deep breath. Old Woman looked around the room. Utnapishtim was sitting up, alert, his eyes fixed on Gilgamesh. Urshanabi was on the edge of his seat, his mouth gaping. They were so hungry for the confrontation, for the blood and mangled body parts. She shook her head in dismay.

Gilgamesh continued with his story. He closed his eyes as he spoke, remembering.

"I'd never seen a creature so large. Black, big—bigger than any creature anywhere. He dwarfed us in size. We were like tiny ants in front of him. And he stank. His musty stench of sweat and filth was overpowering. He gnashed his teeth. He roared. He snarled. He shook his head menacingly from side to side. He showered us with his spittle. Smoke gushed out of his nostrils. He thumped his feet on the ground. My heart pounded."

Gilgamesh opened his eyes and looked at Utnapishtim.

"He spoke to me first, spewing out venom. 'Go away, Gilgamesh,' he roared. 'Go back where you belong. Leave the Cedar Forest. Are you crazy to try to confront me? I will rip you apart. I will scatter your bloodied and mangled body on the ground. Is that what you want? Is that what you came for?'

"'And as for you, Enkidu,' he said. He turned his enormous head, fixing his fierce stare on Enkidu. 'I knew you when you were a puny, scrawny little thing, running around like a wild animal among the herds. I didn't kill you then because you were too skinny to eat. And now, you good-for-nothing, motherless, fatherless piece of clay! You dare to bring Gilgamesh here to the Cedar Forest to confront me? Be off with you! Get out of here the two of you! You're like a pair of sniveling, frightened little girls. I'll slit your throats, rip apart your bodies. I'll feed your entrails to the vultures.' He delivered his threats. He let out a thunderous roar. He shook his head, splattering us with his spittle."

Gilgamesh paused and looked around the room. He wanted them to share in the terror he faced at encountering Humbaba. It worked. Utnapishtim and Urshanabi leaned forward on the edge of their seats. Gilgamesh's description of Humbaba had whet their appetites to learn more about this fierce monster and his legendary strength. They were anxious to hear the gruesome details.

Old Woman knew nothing good would come of this adventure. From the beginning, she had harbored serious misgivings about the killing of Humbaba. She wasn't convinced Humbaba deserved to die. Far from it. She knew the creature was only performing the task assigned to him by a god. He hadn't harmed anyone. He hadn't gone looking for trouble. Trouble had come looking for him in the guise of Gilgamesh, a foolish young king who didn't know the first thing about the responsibility of kingship; and Enkidu, the lofty interpreter of dreams. The fools! Her face tensed with anxiety as she listened with a sunken heart.

Neither Utnapishtim nor Urshanabi thought far enough ahead. Neither one questioned if Humbaba had posed a genuine threat. Neither one asked if Humbaba deserved to die. Neither one bothered to question if Gilgamesh had seriously considered the consequence of his actions. They showed no concern with the dubious ethics of engaging in an unprovoked attack. But they did show an eagerness to hear the details of the attack.

"You must have been terrified," Utnapishtim said after a short pause.

"I was," Gilgamesh replied. "It was like being stuck in a horrifying nightmare with no way out. The monster was huge. His thighs alone were thicker than my waist. His head was the size of my whole body. And his stench was so strong I thought I was going to gag. Everything about him was terrifying. His presence was

GILGAMESH OF URUK

overwhelming. But it was Humbaba's face that drew the most horror. I can't explain it. He had a face unlike any other face. I've not seen anything like it. It wasn't . . ." Gilgamesh hesitated. "It wasn't . . . fixed. His face was sort of mixed up. Strange. Somehow it kept changing from one image to another, from one hideous face to another."

"How? What do you mean?" Utnapishtim asked, his curiosity aroused.

"I don't know how to describe it," Gilgamesh replied. "It's difficult. All I know is the longer I stared at his face, the more it seemed to change. It wouldn't stop. One hideous image just melted into another before my eyes, each one more terrifying than the image that went before. I don't know if what I was seeing was real or magic. But I couldn't tear my eyes away from the gruesome images that kept changing—one after the other. My feet were rooted to the ground. I felt paralyzed. I was scared. I thought I was going to die for sure. I half suspect Humbaba used this technique as a ploy to attack his victims while they were caught in his hypnotic snare."

"How terrible! That sounds so terrifying. Why didn't you run away?" Urshanabi asked. "I would have turned around and run as far away from there as I could."

The words had no sooner left his lips than a look of remorse swept across his face. Utnapishtim glared at him with a look of disdain. He mouthed the words, "You sniveling coward." Gilgamesh glanced at him out of the corner of his eye, a bemused look of curiosity on his face. And then he turned away. Old Woman grimaced, her face taut with tension.

Gilgamesh ignored the interruption.

"I knew we couldn't turn back," he explained. "We had come too far. And besides," he continued, "I kept thinking about the people of Uruk and what they would say about their king." He shot a glance at Urshanabi to see if he had anything to add. But Urshanabi merely hung his head in shame and seemed intent on studying his sandals.

"It was then I remembered mother's prayers to Shamash," Gilgamesh said. "I prayed to Shamash for his help in defeating Humbaba, reminding him I had done everything according to his wishes. I knew he wouldn't let me down. Enkidu urged me forward. He gave the signal to attack. We shrieked our battle cry. We charged at Humbaba. We were fierce warriors."

Old Woman folded her arms and sat back in her chair, waiting for the blood and gore to begin.

"It was terrifying. Humbaba was fierce. He let out a thunderous roar and stomped his feet on the ground. He was so strong. Each of his steps caused the mountains to split open. He moved toward us in slow and deliberate steps. Somehow, the skies turned black as if to reinforce Humbaba's rage.

"Then, from out of nowhere, a thick fog surfaced. It shrouded our eyes so Enkidu and I could barely see in front of us. We struggled to make out the shape of the monster through the dense fog. Although we couldn't see him, we could smell his presence and hear his feet stomping louder and louder as he moved closer and closer to us. I was sure Enkidu and I were fated to die at the hands of this monster. But then, just as Enkidu had predicted, Shamash rescued us. He granted my prayer."

Gilgamesh let out a sigh of relief. He smiled.

"We heard the roar of the winds before we felt their impact," he said. "It was a loud, thunderous roar that shattered everything in its wake. Shamash had sent powerful winds from all four directions to help us. They were strong enough to paralyze Humbaba's movements. They pinned him down to the ground with a huge force. Enkidu and I stood back and watched as Humbaba thrashed about in a frantic struggle to get free. But as strong as he was, his strength was no match for the fierce winds. He couldn't move. Humbaba was trapped." Gilgamesh paused to take a deep breath.

"Go on, son," Utnapishtim said.

Even from where she sat, Old Woman could hear him breathing heavily. He was barely able to contain his excitement.

"As soon as I realized Humbaba was powerless, I grabbed my knife and leapt on top of his mountainous frame. I was about to thrust my knife into his throat when a strange thing happened."

Gilgamesh paused, reflecting on the events. He bowed his head and shook it in dismay. He sighed. "I regret it," he said, after several minutes of silence had elapsed. "I think it was probably a mistake to do it, but Enkidu insisted."

Gilgamesh looked up at Old Woman, seeking compassion and reassurance in her eyes. But Old Woman refused to give him either. She showed her disgust with the whole episode by leaning back in her chair and scowling. Gilgamesh lowered his eyes and stared at the ground. He shook his head.

"I didn't want to do it, but Enkidu said we had no choice. It was probably a mistake. We shouldn't have done it," he said.

"Done what? What did you do, son? Did you kill Humbaba? Isn't that what you'd set out to do? Isn't that why you went to the Cedar Forest?" Utnapishtim said, frustration evident in his tone.

Gilgamesh hung his head and nodded.

Chapter 9: The Killing

Utnapishtim's jaw dropped. He exchanged a disappointed look with Urshanabi. What's the matter with this boy? He no sooner gets to the exciting part than he stops dead in his tracks. Urshanabi's eyes expressed the same disappointment. They were both frustrated and losing patience with the storyteller. Utnapishtim shrugged his shoulders. He waited for his wife to intervene.

"What happened?" Old Woman asked after a brief pause. "What is it you regret, son? Didn't you go to the Cedar Forest intending to kill Humbaba?"

Gilgamesh nodded.

"So, what happened? What do you regret, son?" She kept probing, hoping he would understand, hoping he would express remorse for his actions.

"I wasn't expecting it," Gilgamesh replied, looking up at her. "I don't think Enkidu was expecting it, either. It came as a shock to the two of us."

Gilgamesh's words faltered. He gulped. "Humbaba began to plead for mercy," he said. His voice was hoarse, speaking barely above a whisper.

"He did what?" she asked.

Gilgamesh nodded. "I'd never seen anything like it. He pleaded with me to show him compassion. 'I'll be your slave,' he said. 'I'll serve only you. Let me live. I'll help you. You can have the Cedar Forest. Only let me live. I'll guard it for you so no one else can get in here. You can have all the cedar trees you want. Only let me live. I'll even cut the trees for you. You can build a temple in honor of Shamash. I'll help you. I'll help you build a new and magnificent palace. Only let me live.' He cried. He pleaded. He begged. I felt sorry for him. I wanted to be lenient. It wasn't easy to see this big

GILGAMESH OF URUK

monster begging and pleading. I wanted to be kind. I felt sorry for him. I told Enkidu. Maybe we should let him live. We've subdued him. He's promised to help us. Maybe we should let him live."

Gilgamesh stopped speaking. He buried his face in his hands, overpowered with grief.

Old Woman sensed his struggle. She had suspected all along the encounter with Humbaba would not end well. Although her sympathy for him had long since eroded, she knew it was important for the boy to get the words out, regardless of the difficulty he faced in confronting his error in judgment.

"What happened next, son?" she prompted him.

"Enkidu talked me out of it. He convinced me Humbaba couldn't be trusted," Gilgamesh said, looking up at her with his tear-stained face. "'You can't trust him,' he said. 'You'll never find your way back to Uruk if you let him live,' he warned me. 'Humbaba will make it impossible for you to get home. He'll hunt you down. He'll kill you. You must go for the kill. Don't allow your compassion to get the better of you. Don't give in to the monster,' he said.

"Humbaba heard his words and lashed out at him. 'What an evil creature you are!' he rebuked Enkidu. 'You know the rules of the forest. You know the god Enlil put me here to protect the forest. I had to obey him. If you kill me, you'll bring the anger of the gods upon your heads,' he warned.

"And then Humbaba tried to win Enkidu over by appealing to him directly. 'You and I are much alike,' he said to Enkidu. His voice sounded surprisingly gentle—as if it came from someone else. You wouldn't think such a monster was even capable of speaking so gently. 'We are both motherless and fatherless,' he said. 'We were raised in the wild. And we were both put here for a purpose: you to be a brother to Gilgamesh and me to guard the Cedar Forest for Enlil. So, you see, we have much in common. In many ways, we are like brothers.'

"That was the wrong thing to say to Enkidu. He got so angry. He was repulsed by the monster, angered by any suggestion of similarity between them.

"'How dare you claim we are like brothers?' he yelled. 'You and I are nothing alike. You're a monster—an evil, disgusting monster. I'm a man. I'm the brother of Gilgamesh. I live in a civilized city. You . . . you're nothing! You live in the wild. You're nothing but an animal. You deserve to die.' He shouted. He spat. He brandished his knife at Humbaba while he spoke.

"Humbaba refused to give up. 'I could have killed you many times over,' he reminded Enkidu. 'But I didn't. I showed you mercy. I let you live. Now it's your turn to show me mercy.'

"Enkidu wasn't moved. 'Kill Humbaba,' he beseeched me. 'Do it quickly before Enlil realizes what's happening. Kill him and establish your fame. You'll be known as Gilgamesh, King of Uruk, the brave warrior who killed Humbaba of the Cedar Forest. People will honor you. Your name will live in their minds forever.'

"Humbaba tossed and twisted, struggling to get free. But it was useless. The winds held him down. He let out a huge, guttural roar. Chills went down my spine. Spewing spittle at us, he uttered his curse.

"'I curse you both,' he howled. He looked up at the sky, appealing to the gods. 'May Enkidu die a painful death,' he prayed. 'And may Gilgamesh live the rest of his days wandering the earth in search of consolation for a heart broken by the loss of his beloved. And may he never, ever find peace.'"

Gilgamesh took a deep breath.

"His words struck terror in my heart," he said, speaking in a hoarse whisper. He shuddered, remembering Humbaba's words. The monster's curse had come true. Enkidu had died a painful death. And he, Gilgamesh, was now inconsolable. He buried his face in his hands. He stifled a sob.

He looked up at Old Woman, once again seeking the compassion in her eyes.

"I should have listened to him," he said to her, his eyes pleading for understanding and forgiveness. "I should have shown Humbaba mercy. Instead, I listened to Enkidu. Enkidu was my brother. We had been through so much together. How could I go against his wishes?"

Gilgamesh wrung his hands in despair.

"But perhaps . . . perhaps if I had let Humbaba live, perhaps if I had shown mercy, the gods wouldn't have been angry at us and Enkidu would still be alive today."

Old Woman allowed him a few moments of silence to ponder his words. Perhaps, she thought. Perhaps he's beginning to get an inkling of the consequences of his actions. Maybe he's ready to accept some measure of responsibility—finally.

"I see," she said, tilting her head as if in thought. "You blame Enkidu for Humbaba's death? It was all Enkidu's fault. Isn't that right?"

Gilgamesh nodded.

"Think about it, son. Do you think that's the only reason you killed Humbaba? Because your brother Enkidu told you to do it?"

"Yes, of course. Why? What do you mean?"

"Do you think maybe you had some other reason for killing Humbaba?"

Gilgamesh looked puzzled.

Old Woman leaned forward in her chair and looked into his eyes.

"Didn't you tell us earlier you went to the Cedar Forest because you wanted to establish your name, to be famous?"

Gilgamesh nodded.

"And didn't you say you were determined to kill Humbaba even though he had done nothing to provoke an attack? Do you remember that?"

Gilgamesh stared at her in disbelief. "What are you saying?"

"Well, since you went all the way out there intending to kill Humbaba, and since you now acknowledge maybe your action angered the gods, and since Enkidu is now dead, and . . ."

Gilgamesh interrupted her before she could finish.

"Are you suggesting I'm to blame for Enkidu's death? Is that what you think?"

Fire raged in his eyes. His lower lip trembled as he spoke.

"It doesn't matter what I think, son," she said, leaning back and folding her arms. "What matters is what you think. Do you think you are partly to blame for Enkidu's death?"

Gilgamesh didn't respond. He sat, stunned. His face tensed with anger. His eyes stabbed the old woman with a menacing look. She stared back at him, refusing to flinch, refusing to avert her gaze.

Gilgamesh blinked. He cast his eyes down to avoid looking at her. That he might be responsible for Enkidu's death had never occurred to him. He refused to believe it. He couldn't believe it.

"How could you say that? How could you even say such a thing? Enkidu was my brother. I loved him. I would do anything for him. I told you I wanted to be kind to Humbaba, to let him live. But Enkidu wouldn't let me. It was Enkidu who said we should kill him."

"What difference does it make now who is to blame?" Utnapishtim interjected, a scowl crossing his face. He had lost patience with the direction the dialogue had taken. "The point is that Enkidu is dead. That's all that matters. Get on with your story, son. How did you kill Humbaba?"

Gilgamesh took a deep breath. He avoided looking at the old woman even though he could feel her intense gaze. He was fed up with her probing questions, her unsettling suggestions.

"After I heard Humbaba's curse, I became scared. I dropped my axe. But it was Enkidu . . . Enkidu . . ." He raised his head and looked pointedly at the woman. "Enkidu urged me on. He told me not to listen to the monster's curses. 'Kill him now,' he said. And so I did. I did as Enkidu urged me to do. I lifted my axe and plunged it down on Humbaba's neck with all the strength I had."

Gilgamesh paused. His breathing became labored.

"The cut was deep. The blood gushed out in torrents. You'd think with losing all that blood he would die quickly. But the monster wouldn't die. He struggled. He wreathed. He roared and screeched in agony. I couldn't stand the sounds. I wanted to end it quickly. I heaved my axe. I plunged it at his throat a second time. I heard the sound of crunching bones. But the monster still wouldn't die. His eyes rolled in frenzy. His blood gushed out. He thrashed wildly. It was awful to see. I heaved my axe a third time. I sent it crashing down on him with all my strength. He let out one final roar. That was it. Humbaba was dead."

Utnapishtim and Urshanabi sat back in their chairs and sighed. The description of Humbaba's death had satisfied their thirst for the graphic details.

"I looked at Enkidu," Gilgamesh continued. "We were both splattered with Humbaba's blood. Enkidu smiled. I could tell he was pleased. I won't deny it. I was pleased, too. Actually, I was more relieved than anything. It was awful to watch, awful to hear. I was relieved it was all over."

Gilgamesh fixed his eyes sharply on the woman.

"Humbaba was a monster and he deserved to die," he said emphatically. "And, besides," Gilgamesh scowled as he spoke, "Shamash had helped me to kill him. He sent the winds to hold him down. Not all the gods were angry at us. Some were on my side and wanted the monster dead."

Old Woman didn't respond. Her brow wrinkled into a frown. Utnapishtim, anxious to avoid another lengthy discussion about culpability, prompted Gilgamesh to continue with his story.

"What happened next, son? What did you do after you had killed Humbaba?"

"Enkidu and I split open Humbaba's carcass with our knives. His skin was tough. It took us a long time to cut through. We pulled out his insides. We cut off his head. We dragged it away from his body, laying it against a rock to drain it of blood. The blood still gurgled everywhere. And the smell! What a smell! He stank. Humbaba stank. The putrid stench of his insides made me retch. I had to cover my nose with a rag to stifle the smell. And I couldn't bear the sight of his gaping mouth, protruding sharp teeth, bloodshot eyes. He seemed to be staring straight at me. His eyes followed me wherever I went. Even in death he was a terrifying sight."

Gilgamesh paused. He puffed out his chest, trying to assume an air of confidence.

"We were happy to rid the Cedar Forest of this monster. A monster like that shouldn't be allowed to live. Humbaba deserved to die."

A heavy silence fell on the room. Gilgamesh let the air out of his chest, deflated.

"I don't know what to think any more," he said, shaking his head. "It seemed as if the Cedar Forest didn't share in our happiness. The mountains shook violently when Humbaba roared his death cry. And the blood! There was so much blood. It continued to gush out from his open carcass in torrents. It flooded the nearby valleys.

"And then . . . and then it's as if the sky began to cry," he said in a soft whisper. "A gentle rain fell on the mountains, on the forest, on Humbaba's lifeless carcass, and on us. I don't know. Was the sky washing away all the blood? Was it trying to get rid of every trace of Humbaba? Or was it mourning his death? I don't know. But I sensed it was a bad omen."

Out of the corner of his eye, Gilgamesh saw Old Woman shake her head in dismay. He looked away from her.

"I asked Enkidu about it. He waved away my concerns. Nothing to worry about, he assured me. He was excited. 'Come, Gilgamesh,' he urged me. 'Don't fret about Humbaba anymore. Let's do what we came here to do. Now that we've rid the Cedar Forest of this monster, let's cut down the cedar trees and haul them to Uruk.'

"We took our axes and began chopping down the huge trees. We cut down so many. All the while, Enkidu praised and encouraged me, assuring me my fame would spread beyond Uruk. He suggested we fashion the highest of the trees into a gigantic door for Enlil's temple in Nippur. He wasn't at all concerned about what we'd done. And the more he talked, the more I became convinced we'd done the right thing in killing Humbaba."

Old Woman leaned back in her chair, her eyes fixed sternly on Gilgamesh. She took a deep breath.

GILGAMESH OF URUK

Gilgamesh paused and cast an anxious look in her direction. But she remained silent.

"When we finished cutting down all the trees we needed, we stripped them of their bark. We bound the logs together into a raft. It was a big raft because we'd cut down so many trees. I took a big tree branch and bound it upright at the front of the raft. Enkidu helped me put Humbaba's head on it. After that, we hauled the raft on to the water and floated down the Euphrates, heading for Uruk.

"I was sure the people of Uruk would be impressed by my bravery when they saw the size of the monster's head. I put Humbaba's head to face outwards on the raft so it would be the first thing the people of Uruk would see when we floated into the city. And besides . . . I preferred to see the back of his head. I didn't want to look into Humbaba's eyes."

"Why was that? Why didn't you want to look into his eyes?" Old Woman leaned forward, prodding him with one of her intrusive questions.

Gilgamesh shrugged his shoulders. He ignored her questions.

"We were greeted with huge celebrations when we arrived at Uruk. The people saw Humbaba's head. They couldn't believe how big it was, how fierce his eyes, how sharp his teeth. How did you kill the monster? How did you do it? they asked. Enkidu told them how I had straddled Humbaba's body and thrust my axe into Humbaba's neck in a crashing blow. He told them I showed no fear. The people celebrated. They carried me on their shoulders into the city. There was music and dancing in the streets. Everyone was happy.

"We put the logs to good use. The largest of the cedar logs were used to make a door for Enlil's temple just as Enkidu had suggested. And the rest of the logs were used to build a sturdy wall around the city of Uruk.

People praised me. They said my name would live forever. They were so happy."

Gilgamesh paused, a worried expression on his face. He searched for the right words to say what was on his mind, something that had weighed on him for many days.

"Perhaps," he said, "perhaps . . . Enkidu's death had nothing to do with the killing of Humbaba."

"What do you mean?" Utnapishtim asked.

"Maybe the gods weren't angry at us about that," Gilgamesh reflected aloud.

"Why else would they be angry at you? Why else would they fasten the eye of death on Enkidu? No, son. You're not making any sense. You angered the gods by killing Humbaba. He was put there by the gods to protect the Cedar Forest. And you killed him," Utnapishtim insisted. "That's why Enkidu had to die."

"You said it yourself," Urshanabi chimed in, eager to agree with Utnapishtim. "You said the god Enlil had placed Humbaba to guard the Cedar Forest. And you killed Humbaba. The gods don't take kindly to that sort of thing. Even I know that. They would demand vengeance. Wouldn't the gods demand vengeance?" He looked at Utnapishtim for reassurance.

"That's right," Utnapishtim nodded. "They would insist on a life for a life."

"Well, maybe not. Maybe they took Enkidu because of what happened after we got back to Uruk," Gilgamesh said.

"What? What are you talking about, son? What happened after you got back to Uruk?" Utnapishtim asked. "You didn't do anything wrong. You built a door for Enlil's temple and walls for the city. That wouldn't anger the gods. That would please them. No, son, you're mistaken," he said. "I assure you the gods fastened the eye of death on Enkidu because you killed Humbaba."

"I'm not so sure about that anymore. Maybe Enkidu's death had more to do with the goddess Ishtar," said Gilgamesh. His voice shook.

"The goddess Ishtar? What about the goddess Ishtar?" Old Woman jerked upright in her seat, wondering what foolish thing he had done to offend the goddess.

Gilgamesh hesitated. "I think we may have insulted her," he said after a pause.

"You did what?" Old Woman cried out, baffled by his words. "How? You insulted the goddess Ishtar? I don't believe it! Why, son? What happened? What did you do?"

Gilgamesh caught Old Woman's eyes. He nodded his head.

"Yes," he said, barely above a whisper. "I don't know for sure, but I think Enkidu and I may have offended her."

His listeners stared at each other in stunned silence. The same thought crossed their minds. Only a fool would dare to tangle with the goddess Ishtar. Even Urshanabi had the sense to know you don't provoke the goddess unless you're ready to face her anger. All three turned to Gilgamesh and eyed him with a mixture of curiosity, disbelief, and outright shock.

Chapter 10: The Goddess

"Well, son. You are going to have to explain," Old Woman began after a prolonged, awkward silence. "What did you do? How did you insult her? And why would you do such a stupid thing? It makes no sense to insult a goddess of her stature."

"I'm not sure we did insult her. But I know none of what happened was my fault," Gilgamesh explained, fidgeting nervously in his chair. "I'm not to blame. I wanted nothing to do with her. She came chasing after me," he said, pleading his innocence.

Old Woman shook her head. There he goes, again, she thought. Has the boy learned nothing? Always blaming others for one blunder after another. She caught his eye. He averted her gaze and lowered his eyes.

"Go on, son," she said. "Tell us what happened. Explain what you mean."

"Well," Gilgamesh began, "when we got back to Uruk, I bathed my body. I washed and untangled my hair so it cascaded down to my shoulders. I put oils on my hair, oils on my body. My taut muscles gleamed in the sunlight. I dressed myself in my finest robes. I placed a jeweled crown on my head. I was powerful. I was beautiful. I saw my image reflected in shining armor. I looked so beautiful that the goddess Ishtar desired me."

He looked intently at Old Woman.

"I didn't go after her. She came after me," he insisted, his eyes pleading with her to believe him. "She came to me and offered herself in marriage. She tried to bribe me with gifts."

"Gifts? What sort of gifts?" Urshanabi asked. His interest was piqued. "What did she offer you?"

Old Woman rolled her eyes. What a silly, silly fool! He wants to know all about the gifts. As if the goddess

Ishtar would ever come seeking him to be her spouse. The foolish man! He should know better than to wish for her attention.

"She offered me precious gems, beautiful blue-green eyed servants to please me, a chariot made of lapis lazuli with wheels of gold and horns of amber," Gilgamesh replied. "She promised she would make all her high priests bow down and kiss my feet when I entered her temple. Kings and princes from east and west would honor me and pay tribute. She promised fertility and strength for my animals so they would be the envy of all who saw them. She would do all of this for me and more. All I had to do was agree to take her as my wife."

"And you refused her?" Urshanabi asked, a puzzled expression on his face. "How could you refuse such a delicious offer? How could you say no to all this? She's the goddess Ishtar. I heard she's very beautiful. Why didn't you want her? Didn't you think she was beautiful?"

"Yes, of course she's beautiful," Gilgamesh snapped, his tone mounting with impatience. "But that wasn't the problem."

"Problem? What problem?" Urshanabi asked. "I don't see a problem. I know if the goddess Ishtar ever wanted to marry me, I wouldn't refuse her. I would consent. I would accept all those precious gifts. And I'd be happy to do it. Only a fool would say no to all that."

Urshanabi nodded his head vigorously, turning to Utnapishtim and the woman for reassurance. When none was forthcoming, he clamped his mouth shut and shuffled his feet.

Old Woman looked at Utnapishtim, wondering if he intended to explain to Urshanabi. But he shook his head, cautioning her to say nothing. It was for the best. They knew more about the goddess Ishtar's antics than Urshanabi, but they dared not be openly critical of her.

GILGAMESH OF URUK

Only a fool would criticize her. They left it to Gilgamesh to explain since he'd already offended her, since he'd already paid the price.

"Her gifts were tempting," Gilgamesh said. "And she was very seductive and alluring. But I didn't want to marry her in spite of all that. I had to refuse her." Gilgamesh turned and directed his comments to the old woman.

"You must know what she's like," he said, appealing for understanding. "She's never been loyal to a single one of her lovers. She uses them to satisfy her lust and tosses them aside like fodder for animals when she loses interest. For a while she loved that beautiful young boy, Tammuz. Then she got bored with him. She had him killed and sent to the netherworld. People still grieve his loss and mourn for him from one year to the next."

Old Woman nodded in agreement. She knew all about the stories of the goddess Ishtar and her fickle taste in lovers. She waited, hoping he might recognize something in himself, some similarity in his behavior with the goddess Ishtar's.

"She loved the roller bird until he bored her," Gilgamesh continued. "So she attacked him. Clipped his wings. Now he sits in the woods all day long, weeping for himself. And then there was the lion. Then a stallion. Then a poor shepherd boy who used to bake bread for her. He roasted freshly slaughtered lambs to serve at her table. And how did she repay him for his love? She changed him to a wolf when she got tired of him. Now the shepherd boys who were once his play-mates chase him away. The dogs that used to obey his every command snap at his furry legs."

"Huh!" Urshanabi interjected, surprised by the revelation. "I didn't know this about the goddess Ishtar. I had heard about Tammuz, but I didn't know about any of the others. I didn't know any of this," he repeated, shaking his head in disappointment.

Old Woman chuckled. He's probably thinking he'll stay out of her way to avoid tempting her. As if Ishtar would ever be tempted by Urshanabi! There was no end to these men and their pride. She shook her head in disbelief.

"That's not even all her lovers," Gilgamesh said. He was eager to list the litany of Ishtar's insatiable appetite for lovers. "She loved the gardener, Ishullanu. He brought fresh dates to her table every day. She lusted after him and tried to seduce him. At first, he refused. But she pestered him with her honeyed words until he gave in to her desires. Now he's been turned into a toad. He lives in the same garden he once used to tend. That's what happens to Ishtar's lovers," Gilgamesh concluded with a flourish.

"Yes. What you say is true. The goddess Ishtar is well known for using lovers and tossing them aside," Old Woman said. "Let me ask you something, son."

Gilgamesh squirmed in his chair. Here it comes, he thought. Here comes another one of her pesky questions.

"Did her behavior remind you of anyone?"

"What do you mean?"

"Can you think of someone else who uses lovers only to toss them aside when he's done with them?"

Gilgamesh's eyes widened, flashing with anger, his face turning a fiery red.

"That's different," he said, a noticeable tremor in his voice. "That's completely different. I do it because the gods decreed I should. And, anyway, I don't kill them afterwards. I don't change them into animals. I leave them for their husbands to enjoy."

The old woman opened her mouth to respond when Utnapishtim intervened.

"Did you tell the goddess Ishtar why you refused her?" The boy had shown such little judgment he already suspected his answer.

"Yes, I did. What else was I supposed to do?" Gilgamesh replied, turning his back to Old Woman. "I wanted her to leave me alone. I didn't want to become her lover only to be tossed aside after she'd done with me. Her lust is insatiable. Her taste in lovers is fickle. She discards one lover after another. I told her to go away and leave me alone."

"I'm sure she didn't take it too well," Old Woman said. "People don't like to be reminded of the consequences of their actions."

"No, she didn't take it well at all," Gilgamesh agreed, unaware her pointed comment was directed at him. "She was furious with me. She went to the heavens and cried to her father Anu and her mother Antu. She accused me of thrashing her with foul insults. Her mother tried to reason with her. She suggested maybe she brought it on herself for trying to seduce me. But Ishtar ignored her mother's calm advice. Instead, she pleaded with her father to release the Bull of Heaven. She was determined to hunt me down and destroy my palace. She wanted revenge. Her father refused at first. But in the end, he had to do as she wanted. She threatened to open the gates to the netherworld to release the spirits of the dead if he denied her wishes."

"But that would be a disaster!" Utnapishtim was aghast. "If the dead were released from the Deep, they would cause chaos. They would devour the living. No one would be left alive."

"I know," Gilgamesh said. "But she was determined to punish me, no matter the cost. Anu knew releasing the Bull of Heaven would lead to seven years of famine for Uruk. Ishtar assured him she had stored enough grain in her temple to feed the people for seven years and more.

So father Anu summoned the Bull of Heaven. He handed his daughter the reins. She led the Bull down to earth. She turned him loose with instructions to kill me and destroy my palace. And that's when it began. That's when the battle began."

Gilgamesh paused. He buried his face in his hands. He looked up and directed his words at the old woman.

"We had no choice," he began. "We had to defend ourselves. The Bull of Heaven was fierce. He caused one catastrophe after another. He bellowed loudly as soon as he reached Uruk. With his bellows the earth shook, causing the streams and marshes to dry up. Even the water level of the Euphrates dropped by about ten feet. And then the bull snorted. With his first snort, the earth split open. One hundred of our warriors fell into the crevice and died. With his second snort, the earth split open again. This time two hundred of our warriors fell into the crevice and died. With his third snort, he managed to entrap Enkidu. My poor Enkidu! He fell into the crevice. He was buried up to his waist. Somehow, he managed to free himself. He grabbed the Bull of Heaven by its horns."

Old Woman sighed. Here we go with more senseless killing, she thought. Out of the corner of her eye she saw Urshanabi perched on the edge of his seat, almost frothing at the mouth with excitement. His eyes were fixed on Gilgamesh, mesmerized by his words. Gilgamesh, too, was caught up in describing the action. He spoke hurriedly, one sentence tumbling after the next.

"The Bull of Heaven tried to toss off Enkidu. He shook his head wildly from side to side. He showered Enkidu with his slobber and spittle. And then he lifted his tail and secreted dung. Enkidu was hanging on to the bull's horns for dear life. The bull turned around and swung Enkidu in the dung, smothering his whole body.

GILGAMESH OF URUK

It was disgusting. I rushed up to help my brother. I urged him not to give up. Together we will be victorious, I said. Enkidu and I worked as partners. We attacked. I stabbed the bull until he fell."

Gilgamesh sat up in his chair and looked around the room.

"Yes?" Utnapishtim said.

Satisfied he had captured their attention, Gilgamesh continued with his story.

"We worked well together. Enkidu lifted the bull's tail. He set his foot on his haunch, keeping the bull relatively steady. I charged up to the bull, again. I stabbed him between the shoulders with one fierce jab of my knife."

As he spoke, Gilgamesh moved his arm in a forward motion to demonstrate the thrust of his knife.

"The bull died instantly. We slashed through his thick skin. We tugged and cut until we got to his heart. We yanked it out. We held it up and offered it to Shamash. We had killed the Bull of Heaven."

Gilgamesh sat back in his chair, panting heavily as if to catch his breath from all the excitement.

"I'm guessing the goddess Ishtar was not at all pleased," Old Woman said.

"Ha!" Gilgamesh scoffed. "Pleased? Not exactly! She was furious. She climbed to the top of Uruk's great wall. She showed her displeasure by wreathing in agony. She cried out for all to hear. 'Gilgamesh has slandered me. And now he has killed the Bull of Heaven that was sent to punish him,' she wailed. She looked so helpless and pathetic. I couldn't help but laugh at her. Enkidu went even further. He ripped out one of the bull's thighs and flung it at Ishtar, hitting her in the face."

His listeners gasped.

"What? He did what? He threw a thigh at Ishtar? Why would he do such a thing?" Old Woman was not alone in being horrified at such callous and stupid behavior.

"Well, he did it. He flung the bull's thigh at Ishtar's face," Gilgamesh replied, barely able to conceal his smile. "She deserved it. And then he taunted her with words.

"'If ever I get my hands on you,' he said to her, 'I will rip your body apart the way I have ripped apart the bull. I'll decorate your body with the bull's bloody entrails. You don't deserve anything better.'"

Gilgamesh tried to suppress the urge to laugh, remembering his friend's blustering words.

Old Woman's jaw dropped. She was speechless. She couldn't believe anyone would be stupid enough to insult a goddess in this way. She turned to Utnapishtim and saw a shocked expression on his face. He cast his eyes to the ground in disbelief.

Utnapishtim lifted his head and spoke.

"What happened next, son?" he asked, his voice subdued.

"Then we celebrated," Gilgamesh said, oblivious to the concern he had aroused in his listeners. "Ishtar called for her priestesses. She placed the bull's thigh on the altar. She and her priestesses began to mourn. We ignored their tears and their wailing," said Gilgamesh. "They were pathetic. They couldn't do anything to us."

The smirk on Gilgamesh's face was evident. He felt no remorse for his actions.

"And besides," he continued, "we were too busy admiring the bull's horns. They were gigantic horns of lapis lazuli. Each horn was over two inches thick. Each carried over two hundred gallons of oil. I gave instructions for the oil to be used to anoint the statue of my guardian father, Lugalbanda. And as for the horns—well, they were so beautiful. I hung them on my palace wall so I could admire them."

Gilgamesh paused, expecting his listeners to show an interest in the Bull of Heaven, in his appearance and horns. And somewhere in the back of his mind, he hoped they would join him in laughing at Ishtar's reaction. He needed reassurance. He was beginning to feel a twinge of guilt at insulting the goddess. But his listeners did nothing to assuage his guilt. They remained silent, lost in their own thoughts.

Old Woman stared at him, dumbfounded by his stupidity, a blank expression on her face. Utnapishtim avoided looking at him, his head bowed. And Urshanabi, sensing the tension in the room, decided now would be a good time to study his sandals again.

Hearing nothing from his audience, Gilgamesh continued with his story, determined to make a valiant effort to couch the whole incident in glorified terms.

"Enkidu and I washed ourselves in the river. We held hands as we walked back to the palace. We got into one of my chariots and drove through the streets of Uruk. People were dancing and singing and celebrating our victory over the Bull of Heaven. The atmosphere was festive."

"Festive, you say?" Old Woman asked.

"Yes, of course it was festive," Gilgamesh replied. "Enkidu and I were elated. The singing girls danced around our chariot in celebration. I called out to them. Who is the handsomest of men? And the girls shouted back, 'Gilgamesh is the handsomest of men.' I asked, who is the bravest of men? And the girls replied, 'Enkidu is the bravest of men.' Enkidu and I laughed and laughed. We embraced each other. It was glorious. We had saved the city by killing the Bull of Heaven.

"We were so proud of ourselves. We couldn't resist mocking the goddess. She had sent the Bull of Heaven to defeat us. Instead of killing us, we killed him. We flung his thigh at her face. We wanted to teach her a lesson not to mess with us. And now she had no one to defend her. We were thrilled. We celebrated our victory by feasting all night long."

"You wanted to teach the goddess Ishtar a lesson?" Old Woman asked, her tone incredulous.

Gilgamesh nodded. He looked up at his listeners, his gaze sweeping across their faces, hoping to see congratulatory smiles. He looked surprised to see their somber expressions.

"We didn't do anything wrong," he said, defensively. "We had a right to celebrate. Everyone was celebrating with us. If we had done something to offend the gods, would the people be dancing and singing in the streets?" he asked.

His eyes searched their faces for an answer. But his listeners said nothing. The tension in the room was palpable. Gilgamesh waited in silence. Finally, he asked in dismay, "What's wrong? Is anything wrong? Why are you all looking at me like that? Did we do something wrong?"

Chapter 11: The Revenge

No one answered him right away. And then Utnapishtim spoke up.

"Do you think that was wise, son?" he asked.

"What? Do I think what was wise?" Gilgamesh said, half suspecting yet half refusing to believe he had done anything wrong.

"Do you think it was wise of you to behave the way you did after killing the Bull of Heaven?" Old Woman said.

"But we had to kill him," Gilgamesh insisted. "Ishtar had sent him to kill me and destroy my palace. I had to defend myself. He was killing my people. It was either him or us."

"I understand that," Old Woman said. "But killing him to defend yourself and your city is one thing. Insulting the goddess Ishtar. Taunting her with your words. Flinging the bull's thigh in her face . . . well . . . that's quite another."

"What? What do you mean?" Gilgamesh said. "I don't understand." He stumbled over his words. He had a nagging suspicion it had probably been a mistake to insult the goddess, but until now, no one had dared to confirm his suspicion.

Old Woman turned to Utnapishtim. Her eyes beseeched him for help. Perhaps the boy would be more open to recognizing his foolishness if he heard it from another man instead of from her, she thought.

Utnapishtim caught her eyes. He knew what she wanted. He was reluctant to intervene. The damage had been done and there was no reversing it. But he had no choice. Gilgamesh insisted on an explanation.

"I don't understand," he repeated. "You say I was justified in defending myself, in killing the Bull of

Heaven. What did I do wrong? What did Enkidu and I do wrong?" he asked, looking directly at Utnapishtim.

"You insulted the goddess," Utnapishtim said finally. "You flaunted the defeat of the Bull of Heaven in her face. It would have been wiser to show some humility, son."

"Humility? Why? How? What do you mean?"

"There are more prudent ways of behaving toward the gods after you've angered them," Old Woman said.

Gilgamesh appeared perplexed. He turned to Utnapishtim again, seeking an explanation. Utnapishtim sighed in frustration. Why can't the boy understand? He shook his head in dismay. It should be obvious to him.

"Look, son," he began. "No one is faulting you for defending yourself. But when you kill the Bull of Heaven, an action you know will anger the goddess and probably some of the other gods, you don't go flaunting your victory by dancing and singing and insulting her. You don't fling the bull's thigh in her face. You humiliated her in public. You added insult to injury. That was a big mistake, son. You should have shown some humility."

"You think it's because of how we behaved with her that the gods fastened the eye of death on Enkidu?" His voice faltered. He wanted to know and yet he didn't want to know.

"Probably."

"That and, of course, the killing of Humbaba," Old Woman added.

"Humbaba?" Gilgamesh asked. The anger in his voice was palpable. "Why are you bringing him up again? I told you the gods were on my side when we killed Humbaba," he insisted. "Shamash even helped me by sending the winds to trap Humbaba. And, anyway, mother said it was Shamash's fault I was born with such a restless heart."

The anger in his voice became more pronounced with each sentence he spoke.

"Son," Old Woman sighed in exasperation. "Ninsun is your mother. No mother readily admits to her son having any faults. It's not surprising she would find a way to blame someone else for your actions. The gods told you to subdue Humbaba. Shamash told you to overpower him. And you did. But when Humbaba was caught in your clutches, he begged you for mercy. You said yourself he pleaded with you. He promised to serve you, to cut down the trees in the Cedar Forest for you. What more did you want?

"You subdued him. You had Shamash's blessing to do that much. There was no need to go any further. No need to kill him. The gods had said nothing about killing him. But you killed him even after he begged for his life. After he promised to serve you. That was a mistake, son. You should have been merciful, shown compassion. Instead, you butchered him."

She paused, taking a deep breath. "I am sure that, too, angered the gods, just as your insults to Ishtar angered them."

A dejected Gilgamesh bowed his head in silence. "But . . . but . . ." He stuttered. His voice trailed off trying to find the right words.

Old Woman looked at him. Against her better judgment, her heart went out to the poor foolish boy. Even though he was naïve, arrogant, and incorrigible, she felt sorry for him. She turned to Utnapishtim, inclining her head toward Gilgamesh to indicate it was his turn to say something. But Utnapishtim shrugged his shoulders. He averted her gaze. That husband of mine is useless, she thought. He wouldn't know how to console a distraught individual even if you hit him on the head with the instructions. She glanced at Urshanabi, hoping he might be able to say something comforting to the young man as one man to another. But one look at Urshanabi while he fumbled with his sandals told her he, too, was useless. There was no way around it. It was left up to her.

"It's all right, son," she began. "Don't be upset. The gods are fickle. They'll do to us as they will. Sometimes we don't even know why they do what they do. The most we can hope for is to stay out of their way and tread very carefully around them."

"But why did they have to take Enkidu from me?" Gilgamesh sobbed.

"Well, what did you expect them to do?" she replied, exasperation creeping into her voice. "You angered them. You killed Humbaba. You showed no compassion when he begged for mercy. And if that weren't bad enough, you insulted the goddess Ishtar. The gods don't take to such things kindly. They insist on revenge. One of you had to pay. One of you had to die. And it couldn't be you because you're part god. You're one of them. They're not going to turn against one of their own. There was no one left but Enkidu. Enkidu had to die."

Gilgamesh choked back a sob. "What should I have done?" he said, speaking barely above a whisper, his voice feeble.

Old Woman stared at him intently, frustration scrawled across her face. Either he doesn't get it or he doesn't want to get it, she thought. She heaved a sigh and tried again.

"To begin with, son, it would have been better for you to have shown compassion to Humbaba. You should have let him live. That would have pleased the gods. And secondly, although you had no choice but to defend yourself against the Bull of Heaven, you should have respected the goddess Ishtar. You should have gone on your knees and begged her forgiveness after you killed him."

Gilgamesh sat up with a jerk.

"Gone on my knees? Begged Ishtar's forgiveness?" he asked, raising his voice. He was incredulous. "Why should I ask for her forgiveness? She came after me. She tried to seduce me. And when I rejected her offer, she turned the Bull of Heaven loose to kill me, to destroy my palace, to kill my people. She should go down on her knees and beg me for forgiveness!"

"As you wish, son," Old Woman sighed. "But you should know by now it doesn't work that way with the gods. Enkidu is dead, isn't he?"

Gilgamesh nodded. He buried his face in his hands, sobbing quietly.

"That night," he stammered after several minutes. "That night, after we had done celebrating, we slept. When I woke up, I saw Enkidu staring at me. I asked him what was wrong. 'I have had a terrifying dream,' he told me."

Old Woman sat up. "Another dream. What was this one about?"

"He dreamt our actions had angered the gods. He dreamt the gods held a council meeting. Anu was angry. He told the gods we had killed Humbaba, killed the Bull of Heaven. He raised his voice. His shouts echoed in the chamber. They have to pay with their lives, he insisted. One of them must die. The gods argued. Enkidu said Shamash tried to defend us. But Enlil overruled him. The gods agreed. One of us had to die. Enlil said it must be Enkidu. Enkidu must die. Gilgamesh should live. All the gods shouted with one voice, 'Enkidu must die.'" Gilgamesh paused. "That was when Enkidu woke up. That was his dream. That's all he could remember."

His voice trailed off. Then he fell silent.

Old Woman felt vindicated. Her intuition had been right. The gods were angry at the senseless killing of Humbaba and the insults to the goddess Ishtar. And now

Enkidu's dream proved her correct. She glanced at Utnapishtim. He nodded his head in acknowledgement.

"What happened next?" she asked Gilgamesh.

"I didn't want to believe it. I refused. Enkidu told me he was dying. He said he would soon be joining the dead in the netherworld. He would never see me again. I couldn't accept it. I told him he was being foolish. I told him he was misinterpreting his own dream. I tried to encourage him. But then he had a second dream."

"Yes?" Old Woman said, anticipating another validation.

"This time he dreamt he was standing alone on a grassy meadow. The heavens and earth spoke to each other in thunderous voices. Suddenly a fierce creature loomed from the sky. He had the head and paws of a lion, the wings and talons of an eagle. The creature swooped down on Enkidu. It seized him by the hair. It jumped on top of him. It kept jumping and jumping. It crushed his bones.

"Enkidu said he cried out to me in his dream for help. I didn't help him. I was too afraid to come forward. The creature touched Enkidu. He watched in horror as his arms covered with feathers. He said he tried to scream but no sounds came out of his mouth. Then the creature tied Enkidu's arms behind his back. Enkidu kicked and struggled all the while. But the creature didn't let go. It dragged him down to the Deep."

Gilgamesh shuddered and took a deep breath.

"He described the netherworld. It was dark. There were others there. Those who had gone before him in death. All were clothed in bird-like feathers. Their food was dirt; their drink was clay. The door was locked—a heavy bolt, thick with dust. There was no way out. Enkidu saw kings and princes, high priests and priestesses, devotees and prophets. All looked the same.

All treated the same. All squatted in the darkness of the netherworld. And then he saw her."

Gilgamesh came to an abrupt stop. He wrapped his arms around his chest and began swaying gently back and forth.

Urshanabi caught his breath, shuddering.

"Who?" Utnapishtim asked. "Who did he see?"

Gilgamesh ignored the question. He continued to sway back and forth.

"Who did he see? Utnapishtim repeated his question.

"He saw Queen Ereshkigal, the Queen of the Deep," Gilgamesh whispered after a brief pause. His voice quivered, his body shook.

A cold chill descended on the room at the mention of her name.

"Squatting beside Ereshkigal was Belet-Seri, she who records in the Book of Death for the gods. When Ereshkigal saw Enkidu, she called out, 'Who is this new resident to my kingdom?' Enkidu said her voice crackled. It was deep, harsh, and cold as death. And that is when Enkidu woke up from his second dream. His body was shivering even though he was covered in sweat. He was terrified. So was I."

Gilgamesh's description was followed by a long silence. Each of his listeners was visualizing the encounter with Ereshkigal in the Deep.

Old Woman uttered a silent prayer, thanking the gods for granting her and Utnapishtim their gift of eternal life. No matter how challenging eternal life might be, she thought, no matter the horrors they were forced to witness before receiving eternal life, at least it was preferable to the alternative. *I must stop grumbling aloud about our situation,* she reminded herself. *This has to be better than the netherworld.*

Urshanabi was the first to break the silence that had enveloped the room.

"That's a scary dream. Enkidu must have been horrified," he said, his voice quaking.

"He was," Gilgamesh said. "Enkidu was white, his face drained of blood, his heart pounding. I, too, was so scared for my brother. But I dismissed the dream. I refused to believe the gods would take him away from me. I made excuses. I tried to convince him it might be a good omen since the gods sometimes send terrifying dreams to healthy men. They're trying to make you stronger, I said. I argued it might even be a sign he was recovering.

"I did everything I could to assure him. I promised to pray to Shamash, to Anu, to Enlil, to Ea. I promised to pray to all of them. I promised to beg for forgiveness. I promised to make a gold statue in his image to restore him to good health. But Enkidu told me all my efforts were useless. The gods had made up their minds. Enlil would not retract his decision. Nothing would cure Enkidu of his illness. Death had fastened its grip on him. His fate was sealed."

Tears welled up in Gilgamesh's dark eyes and streamed down his face. He buried his face in his hands, weeping openly and without embarrassment.

Chapter 12: The Death

Old Woman glanced at Utnapishtim. He leaned back in his chair. He looked exhausted. A heavy silence shrouded the room. No one spoke. No one knew what to say. They waited in silence for Gilgamesh to speak. It was obvious to them he wasn't finished with his story yet. The old woman stood up and fetched him another cup of water. Gilgamesh gulped it down. He managed to compose himself and resume his story.

"It tore me apart," he began. "I'd never seen anything like it. Enkidu became very ill. He was in a lot of pain. He couldn't stop weeping. He was bitter. He lashed angrily against all those responsible for tearing him away from his former life in the wilderness. He blamed the two people who had played a role in his change. He cursed the trapper. He asked Shamash to destroy his livelihood. 'May he never be successful in trapping animals. May he starve to death for bringing me here,' he cried out.

"His words against the trapper were strong. But it was for Shamhat, Ishtar's priestess, he reserved his most scathing words."

"Shamhat? Why Shamhat?" Old Woman interrupted him. "All she did was help him. You sent her there to do her job. She did it. Why would he attack her?"

"He lashed out at her for introducing him to civilization and city life," Gilgamesh said. "He blamed her for seducing him away from his former life in the wilderness. He had once been happy there, roaming innocent and free. He cursed Shamhat with bitter, strong words. He wished for her a loathsome fate."

"What did he say?" Old Woman was concerned. Curses held a certain power, regardless of who uttered them. Shamhat had nothing wrong. She was being blamed for doing her job.

"Enkidu showered her with curses, one worse than the other. 'May you never find the security of a home and family,' he said. 'May you remain childless all your life. May you be beaten. May you be rejected in favor of younger and prettier girls. May you never possess anything of beauty. May your roof leak. May wild dogs and owls inhabit your home. May drunken men foul your body with their vomit. May you be forced to conduct your business near a tavern wall. May wives reject you and taunt you. May you walk barefoot until thorns and briars tear at your feet causing them to bleed. May you be mocked and ridiculed and beaten wherever you go. And may you never find peace.'"

Old Woman was horrified.

"That's awful! How could he say all that? What a horrible curse!" she gasped. "Enkidu was harsh and cruel and ungrateful! After everything Shamhat had done for him, this is how he repays her? Your Enkidu was an ungrateful wretch!"

"Yes, but . . ." Gilgamesh tried to interrupt.

She wouldn't allow him to edge in any more words. She forced him to hear her out.

"Enkidu was ungrateful," she said, her voice quaking. "He cursed the poor woman with a cruel fate. A curse is not an easy thing. It has power. He had no right to say these things to her. Poor Shamhat! He was wrong. He was an ungrateful wretch, your Enkidu," she repeated, shaking her head vigorously.

She scowled, staring intently at him, defying him to contradict her.

"Imagine inflicting such a nasty curse on the poor woman when all she did was perform her duty as a priestess of the goddess Ishtar." Her face burned with indignation.

"Yes, I know it was wrong of him," Gilgamesh said. "I know he went too far. I'm trying to explain but you won't let me. Enkidu took the curse back right away," he said hurriedly. "He retracted the curse when Shamash prompted him to consider all he owed to Shamhat.

"Shamash reminded him how Shamhat had taught him to eat and drink at a table with civilized men. He reminded him he no longer had to forage for food with wild animals. She had introduced him to bread and wine, food grown and cultivated by humans. She had clothed him in fine garments whereas in the past he had only his skin and hair to protect him from the bitter cold. And, most importantly, she had brought him to the glorious city of Uruk where he met me and became my brother."

Gilgamesh paused and looked up at the old woman. He had captured her attention.

"Enkidu was reminded of all the benefits, all the respect he received because he was my companion and brother. Shamash reminded him without Shamhat, none of this would have been possible."

"Enkidu agreed. He immediately took back the curse. He wished for Shamhat a life of riches and glory. He wished princes, kings, and nobles would seek her from miles around to become her lovers. He asked she be showered with precious gifts of carnelian, gold, and lapis lazuli. He wished for her generous lovers whose one desire would be to lie naked by her side, men who would be willing to abandon their wives and children for a moment's glory with her."

Gilgamesh's words tumbled out without pause. "You see," he said, looking at the old woman. "Enkidu was a good man. He really didn't mean any harm to come to Shamhat. He was just upset. He was in a lot of pain. That's all."

Old Woman stared at him. Was he sincere in what he said or was he just stringing words together to redeem his friend, she wondered. She stared long and hard.

Gilgamesh held her gaze without squirming in his seat or looking guilty. She was satisfied he told the truth. After all, she thought, there wouldn't be much point in lying to me. She sighed. Her face relaxed.

"That's more like it," she said.

She folded her arms and leaned back in her chair.

"Shamhat should be honored and showered with gifts, not tossed out and treated like a piece of rotten meat. I'm glad Shamash put him right. But it still doesn't speak highly of your friend. He was too quick to forget how much he owed the priestess of Ishtar, too quick to blame someone else for his misfortune."

Gilgamesh ignored her comment.

He must be made to understand, she said to herself. Sooner or later, he has to realize the truth. He has to know no one was to blame for Enkidu's death other than Enkidu and possibly one other person. Old Woman looked up at him, wondering if he even suspected his role. But he was too busy wrapped up in his thoughts of Enkidu's final days to pay her any heed.

"Enkidu endured a terrible agony during the last twelve days of his life," Gilgamesh said. He spoke slowly in hushed tones, his voice hoarse. His listeners had to lean forward to hear him.

"He became very ill. He was in so much pain. His body writhed in agony the whole time. His face twisted and contorted. He couldn't get any relief from the pain. I stayed by his side. I could do nothing to ease his agony."

Gilgamesh fidgeted in his chair. Anxiety crept into his voice as he wrung his hands in despair.

"At one point, Enkidu forced himself to sit up. He called out to me, 'Gilgamesh, my brother, where are you? Have you abandoned me? You promised to stay with me. You promised to help me fight off this peril. Have you left me forever?'

"I was right by his bedside. He couldn't see me. I tried to comfort him. But by then he could neither see me nor hear me. He had already begun to take his leave from this world.

"Enkidu's agony lasted for twelve days. Twelve long days. Twelve grueling days. His screams of pain got worse with each day. I couldn't bear to hear it. I wanted to run away so I wouldn't have to hear it any more. But I stayed by his side. I stayed until the very bitter end. I stayed until I heard the death rattle in his throat. My Enkidu was gone."

Gilgamesh tried to choke back the flood welling up in his eyes. But it was no use. The tears streamed down his cheeks. He wept bitter tears.

Old Woman went to him and gently stroked his shoulder for comfort.

"I begged him not to leave me," he said, gasping for breath in between sobs. "Enkidu, don't leave me, my beloved. Don't leave me. I wept by his bedside all night. At dawn, I summoned the counselors of Uruk. I cried out my lament for Enkidu. I wanted the whole world to share in my grief for him, to hear me weep for my beloved," he cried, his words punctuated by sobs.

"I reminded them Enkidu came from the wilderness. He had lived with animals. I called upon all to mourn his fate. I called out to the wild animals; to the citizens of Uruk; to the trees of the Cedar Forest; to the paths Enkidu and I had walked; to the rivers we crossed; to the mountains we climbed; to the trees we cut down; to the shepherds, the farmers, the priestesses of Ishtar; and to everyone else I could remember. I wanted them to weep with me," Gilgamesh said, tears streaming down in torrents. "I declared I would love him and mourn for him as long as I lived. I would feel his loss like a mother feels the loss of her child, like a lover feels the loss of his beloved. I will never, ever forget him."

He paused to catch his breath, burying his face in his hands. "I knew he was dead, but I couldn't let him go," Gilgamesh sobbed.

He looked up at the old woman, searching her face. Tears burned her eyes as she watched him. She returned his look with compassion. A tear trickled down her face. She brushed it aside, hurriedly. She knew what it meant to experience loss in life. She had suffered from it. She knew how much pain it brought. In spite of all his foolishness, she found herself feeling sorry for the young man in his grief.

"I didn't want to believe he was gone," Gilgamesh said. "I called out to him. I reminded him of our adventure to the Cedar Forest, of how we had been victorious in killing the monster Humbaba, of how we had fought together and killed the Bull of Heaven. I put my hand on his heart. It had stopped beating. I veiled his face like a bride. I didn't know where to go, what to do. I paced up and down near his bed. I felt trapped like an animal."

Gilgamesh stood up abruptly and started pacing the room. His fists were clenched. Words stumbled out of his mouth.

"I ripped out clumps of my hair. I tore off my robes. I refused to let him go. I thought if I clung to him long enough and hard enough, he would come back to me. I wept by his side for six days and seven nights. And then . . . and then I saw a horrible sight. I saw a maggot crawling out of his nose. Ugh! It was awful."

Gilgamesh stopped pacing. His body shivered. He shrugged it off, shaking his head as if to dispel a negative thought.

"That's when I knew Enkidu had left me forever. He had gone to the Deep," he said. "There was nothing more I could do. I could never bring him back."

He walked slowly back to his seat. He slumped down on his chair and took some deep breaths.

"The next morning, I ordered a statue to be built of my beloved Enkidu. It was to be more splendid than any statue ever made. Its beard was to be made of lapis lazuli, its chest made of gold. His barge was to be made of obsidian and gems of every color. It was to be piled high with silver and gold.

"I opened up my treasury, bringing out weapons and tools with handles of jewels, ivory, and gold. I butchered oxen and sheep on Enkidu's behalf. I piled gifts to the gods of the Deep. I wanted them to welcome my friend to the dwelling place of the dead. To Shamash, I gave a carnelian bowl filled with honey and a lapis lazuli bowl filled with butter. To Ishtar, it was a polished javelin of cedar so she would love Enkidu as I loved him and allow him to walk by her side in the Deep as he had walked by my side in Uruk. To Sin, the god of the moon, I offered a knife made of a carved obsidian blade. And to Ereshkigal I offered a flask of lapis lazuli. To each of the gods and their helpers I offered precious gifts—to Namtar, Hushbishag, Qassa-tabat, Ninshuluhha, and Bibbu. I asked the gods to accept these gifts on behalf of Enkidu. I asked them to ease his broken heart, to welcome him by their side."

Gilgamesh took a deep breath. He brooded in silence, deep in thought. His listeners remained respectfully quiet, waiting for him to speak.

"After the funeral, I grew my hair out like a wild man. I clothed myself in the skin of a lion. I left Uruk. I headed for the wilderness."

"The wilderness? Why the wilderness?" Urshanabi asked. His tone was brusque. "Why did you go to the wilderness?" he asked. "If I lived in the city, I would never leave it. The city has everything—fun and games and parties. The wilderness has nothing. That's why it's called a wilderness. Hah!" He tossed his head back and laughed. "That's why it's called a wilderness," he repeated, looking around the room, flushed with pride at his joke.

Utnapishtim and the old woman exchanged a look. That Urshanabi! They spoke with their eyes. He had no sensitivity, no tact. He blurts out the first thing that comes to his mind. Old Woman shook her head. She rolled her eyes. She scowled, hoping he would keep his mouth shut. Utnapishtim glared at him. Gilgamesh didn't reply right away. He took a couple of deep breaths.

"I was grieving," he said. "I was lost. I didn't know what to do or where to turn. All I knew was my beloved Enkidu was gone from my side forever. I didn't want to stay in the city. Everywhere I looked I saw reminders of Enkidu, of the time we had spent together. I needed to leave, to get away from there. I wanted to get closer to Enkidu's spirit, to the person he was before he came to the city. I wanted to know the person he was before I met him. So I dressed in animal skins. I grew my hair. I roamed the wilderness with animals just as Enkidu had done before I met him.

"Enkidu's death forced me to question things I'd never given much thought to before. I asked myself, what is the meaning of this life if we're all going to die? Am I to die, too? Am I to die just like my brother, Enkidu? I needed answers. I set off in the wilderness, hoping to find the answers."

"And did you find any answers?" Utnapishtim asked.

"No," Gilgamesh replied. "That's why I'm here. That's why I came seeking you. You're Utnapishtim, the Faraway. You're immortal. The gods granted you everlasting life. I want to know how you got them to do it. I want to know the meaning of life from someone who will never die. I want to know how you cheated death."

"And you think my story will somehow help you?" Utnapishtim asked. "You think you can convince the gods to give you the gift of everlasting life? You think you, too, will be able to cheat death and find the answers you seek?"

"Yes," Gilgamesh said. "I'm willing to try anything. I want to know why we live, why we die. I want to know how I can cheat death. I want to know how you did it."

Utnapishtim shook his head. "Son," he said, "I told you earlier when we were down by the seashore, it doesn't work that way. The gods will grant everlasting life to whomever they please. You can't wrestle it out of them. You're waging a battle you won't win. Go back home, son. Be content with your lot in life."

"How can I be content knowing my fate is to die?" a bewildered Gilgamesh asked. "I've come such a long way to find you. You must help me," he insisted. "I've been on a long journey, a difficult journey. You must help me find answers," he pleaded. "Utnapishtim, please. I beg of you. Tell me. How did you cheat death?"

Old Woman looked at Utnapishtim and nodded. Do what you can to help him, she said with her eyes.

Chapter 13: The Interlude

Utnapishtim shook his head. He didn't know what more he could say to make Gilgamesh understand. He didn't want to disappoint the young man, but he didn't have anything more to offer. He looked at Old Woman hoping she might have a suggestion. She shrugged her shoulders. She didn't know what to offer the young man, either. So Utnapishtim tried again.

"Son, you have to make the most of life while you have it. Only the gods know when death will fasten its grip on you. All any of us know for sure is that life is short."

"But not for you," Gilgamesh retorted. "Life isn't short for you. It's easy for you to say these things because you know you'll never die. You'll live forever. I came all this way to learn know how you did it. How did you convince the gods to grant you eternal life?"

"You're right. Life isn't short for me," Utnapishtim said, his tone resigned. "Old Woman and I will live forever." And then he fell silent, lost in his own thoughts.

An uncomfortable hush descended on the room. The atmosphere bristled with tension. Gilgamesh brooded silently while waiting for Utnapishtim to speak. And for his part, Utnapishtim felt he had said all there was to say. Old Woman decided it was time to intervene, thinking perhaps a temporary distraction might provide them with some relief.

"Well, son," she said after a short pause. "You've certainly been through a lot. And you've talked for quite some time now. Why don't you take a few minutes to relax before you tell us the rest of your story? It's getting late in the day so the sun's heat is no longer at its full strength. Why don't you take advantage of the time?

GILGAMESH OF URUK

Go outside and take a walk. The cool breeze will refresh you."

She turned to Urshanabi. The determined look on her face indicated she would not tolerate any objections from him. To Urshanabi she said, "Urshanabi, go along with him to keep him company."

Urshanabi's jaw dropped. He stared at her, a baffled expression on his face. His first inclination was to protest, to tell her he had no idea what to do with the young man or what to say to him. But one look at her face convinced him he would be better off to keep his reservations to himself. Gilgamesh, too, was puzzled.

"What?" he asked, sitting straight up from his hunched position. "You want me to do what?"

"Go outside. Find a shady spot to sit. Breathe the fresh air. Relax for a little while. You can finish the rest of your story when you get back. Run along, now," she insisted.

"I don't want to go out. I don't need fresh air. I don't need to rest. What I need is to hear your story," Gilgamesh objected.

"Enough!" Old Woman's tone was emphatic. "Run along now and do as I say."

She was smiling, but the look in her eyes showed she would brook no rebuttal.

Gilgamesh didn't respond. He froze in his seat, his head bowed, his eyes fixated on the floor. Old Woman turned to Urshanabi and motioned him to get up. He did so reluctantly and stood in front of Gilgamesh. His arms dangled listlessly by his side. He didn't know what to do to make the young man get up from his chair. Gilgamesh looked up at him with a dazed expression. He stood up slowly. He had lost all will power to argue or object. With a bowed head, he plodded toward the door while Urshanabi shuffled behind him.

As he was about to exit, Urshanabi whispered to Old Woman, his face taut with anxiety, "What are we to talk about? What am I to say to him?"

"It's best if you say nothing at all. If he talks, just listen. And whatever you do, do not offer him any advice," she said emphatically. She watched as they trudged out of the cabin.

Utnapishtim turned to his wife. "Well, what are we to do about him?" he asked. "I'm at a loss."

"He's in very bad shape," she replied. "He's in a lot of pain. But the worst part is he still doesn't seem to grasp both he and Enkidu brought this on themselves. He just shuffles around the issue to avoid facing the truth. Perhaps if he came to terms with his role in Enkidu's death, he might find it easier to cope with his loss. He still talks of the killing of Humbaba as if it were cause for celebration. And he doesn't understand no good can come of hurling insults at the goddess Ishtar."

Utnapishtim nodded his head in agreement. They were silent, lost in thought.

"Of course, Enkidu had to die," Old Woman said, eventually picking up the thread. "There was no way around it. But the poor boy still refuses to accept it or to accept some measure of blame for his death. He sniffs around finding others to blame. He's convinced himself the god Shamash is responsible for his restless spirit. He insists the goddess Ishtar deserved the insults. It's always someone else's fault, never his. It's common knowledge the gods will punish those who defy them or don't show them respect. Why doesn't he understand that?" she asked.

"I don't know. Maybe it's because he is part god. Maybe he thinks the rules don't apply to him. Maybe he views the rules the rest of us mortals have to abide by with nothing but contempt. Maybe he thinks he's better than the rest of us."

"Or maybe because he's still a child," Old Woman said. "I don't know what to make of him." She shook her head in frustration. "One minute I feel sorry for him; the next minute I want to slap some sense into him. I can't understand the boy. Who knows what he really thinks? But in spite of the mess he's made, we should still try to help him."

"How?" Utnapishtim asked. "You heard what I told him. What more I can say to help him? How do I get him to believe me? He refuses to hear me. He just won't accept the fact he can't force the gods to grant him immortality. And to make matters worse, he's arrogant. I sensed that about him from the second he opened his mouth. He thinks he's entitled to special privileges. That's the part god in him, too, I guess."

"Probably," Old Woman agreed. She hesitated. "But I feel sorry for him, all the same."

Neither Utnapishtim nor Old Woman spoke again for several minutes, both lost in thought. Finally, Utnapishtim spoke up.

"You know," he said after a few moments of reflection, "You realize there's more to it than just grief over the loss of Enkidu."

"What do you mean?" she asked. "What more is there?"

"Fear," Utnapishtim replied. "The boy is afraid."

"Afraid? Yes, he's afraid, all right. But I'm not sure of what. Afraid of death?"

"Afraid of the very nature of his existence," Utnapishtim answered. "Afraid of the pains of mortality. Afraid of dying. Afraid of death."

"Afraid of death? He puts on such a show of not being afraid of anything. Why should he be afraid of death?"

"A lot of people are afraid of death."

"But surely not Gilgamesh. He's a fierce warrior." Her tone was laced with sarcasm.

"He's seen so much death. And he of all people has been responsible for the deaths of so many. No, it must be something else."

She shook her head. Shrugging her shoulders, she added, "I don't know. Maybe you're right."

"Think about it. He's seen death before, but in the past, death was something distant. Something that happened to others—to strangers, to people and monsters he didn't care about. Enkidu's death is probably the first time he's had to witness the death of someone he loved. He was forced to confront it. He saw it close-up. He was forced to recognize its inevitability. Death became an intimate reality for him, a reality he's never had to cope with before."

Utnapishtim paused briefly.

"Why do you think he insists on knowing how we cheated death even though I have told him repeatedly our story will not help him get any closer to achieving immortality?"

"Why?" Old Woman asked.

"I suspect it's because he is still trying to find a way out. He hopes to learn something from our story. He wants to apply it to himself, so he, too, can cheat death."

"I thought he just wanted to hear our story of surviving the flood, so he can take it back with him to Uruk."

"That, too. But he also wants to cheat death."

"Why would he want to cheat death? That makes no sense to me. I know I wouldn't want to cheat death," she said emphatically. But then she recalled Enkidu's dream in which he grew bird-like feathers and was locked up in the Deep with no way to escape. A shiver ran down her spine. She swallowed hard.

"That's because you're not going to die," Utnapishtim replied. "The gods blessed you with a gift that is the envy of all mortals."

"So you keep saying. But sometimes I wonder if their gift is a blessing at all," she said, hesitation creeping into her voice. "Sometimes I wonder if, instead, it's a curse," she mumbled.

"What? Hush your mouth, Wife! Don't say that! Don't ever say that aloud again!" Utnapishtim said, shocked to hear her say those words. "The gods may hear you. They gave us eternal life as a gift. You should be thankful."

He spoke in a loud whisper, fearful they might be overheard by one of the gods.

"I am thankful. Well . . ." Old Woman hesitated. "Let's just say I'm thankful most of the time. But sometimes I get so weary of life. Sometimes I think even death, as terrifying as it is, may be preferable to living forever. Sometimes . . ." she paused and looked at Utnapishtim. "Sometimes, I long for the release of death. And sometimes I envy those who died during the great calamity."

"How can you say that?" Utnapishtim asked, bewildered. "You know what we went through to survive, to get to where we are now. Don't you remember how painful the whole ordeal was for us?"

"Remember? How can I forget?" she asked. "I remember the rain, the water, the people grasping at anything to save them from drowning. I can still see them clutching desperately at reeds, at anything that might help them stay afloat. I remember their screams, their pleas for help. I remember our home, our possessions, everything buried in the deluge. I remember it all too well. I wish I didn't. I wish I could forget it."

Her voice trailed off; her eyes gazed into the distance.

"Don't you ever get tired of life, Utnapishtim?" she asked.

"No!" Utnapishtim's response was emphatic. "And neither should you. We're happy here. We have each other. We have the sunlight, the sky. We have water and food. What more could you want? How can you even think you would prefer the darkness and misery of the netherworld to being here?"

"I know. I know," she replied. "But don't you ever miss it?" she asked.

"Miss what?"

"Miss our old home in Shuruppak? Miss being king? Miss our friends? Our family? Miss the community we once had?"

"Yes, I think of it sometimes," Utnapishtim said, a wistful tone creeping into his voice. He reflected for a few minutes and then added, "But it's all gone now. Nothing is the same. I would still rather be here than in the netherworld. We should be thankful to the gods for their gift."

Old Woman didn't respond. She stared into the distance, her mind far away.

Utnapishtim shrugged. "Sometimes I don't understand you at all," he mumbled.

"I know," she said. "Sometimes I don't understand me either. Sometimes I feel so torn." She smiled and was about to say more when their conversation was interrupted.

Gilgamesh and Urshanabi could be heard making their way back to the cabin. Utnapishtim glanced at her. Years of living together had taught them to communicate with their eyes. Without saying a word, they agreed to delay their discussion until they could be alone. The topic was far too sensitive to be discussed in the presence of others.

GILGAMESH OF URUK

Meanwhile, Gilgamesh and Urshanabi had been aimless in their wandering outside. They had walked down to the seashore and gazed out at the water. They had trudged along the water's edge, shuffling the sand under their feet. They had even crouched under a palm tree for a short while to avoid the intense glare of the sun. Neither one of them had spoken, Gilgamesh still brooding, wrapped up in his own thoughts; Urshanabi heeding Old Woman's advice by keeping silent. He was afraid to open his mouth in case the wrong words leapt out.

Without uttering a sound, Gilgamesh abruptly stood up, brushing off the sand from his clothes.

"I've had enough," he announced. "I'm going back. You can stay out here if you want."

He began making his way back to the house. Urshanabi followed in silence. They shuffled into the cabin. Neither looked refreshed. The expression on Urshanabi's face revealed their excursion to the outdoors had done them little good. He was tense. He caught Old Woman's eyes and shrugged his shoulders. He walked slowly across the room and took his seat in the corner.

For his part, Gilgamesh looked despondent and weary, his head bowed, his shoulders hunched, and his feet dragging along the floor.

Old Woman's heart went out to him. The poor boy, she thought. We have to help him. We have to find some way of helping him. She glanced at Utnapishtim. He shook his head to suggest he was baffled by the boy's behavior and had no idea what to do.

"Ah, there you are," she said to welcome them back, injecting a cheerful tone to her voice. "Come and sit down. How do you feel, son? Any better?"

Gilgamesh caught her eyes, a glazed expression on his face. She spoke encouragingly to him.

"Son, why don't you finish your story?" she urged him. "Tell us how you got here. It must have been a very difficult journey. You said you had to overcome many obstacles. What sort of obstacles? Utnapishtim and I came here by a different route. We're interested to hear about your journey. Tell us how you did it. How did you find us? Did anyone help you?"

When Gilgamesh didn't respond, she spoke again.

"Come along, son," she insisted. "We're all anxious to hear the rest of your story."

Gilgamesh looked up at her. He didn't feel like speaking, his body fatigued, his eyelids heavy. But he felt he owed them an explanation. They had welcomed him into their home. They had shown him kindness. They had fed him. They had listened to him. It seemed only right to entertain them with what they wanted to hear. Perhaps if I finish telling them my story, he said to himself, they might tell me theirs. He took a deep breath and resumed his story.

Chapter 14: The Scorpion People

"I started my journey after leaving Uruk by heading east. I trekked over grasslands and wilderness. My heart was heavy, my feet weary. I felt as if I had spent my whole life dragging one foot after another. At long last I arrived at the Twin Peaks."

"The Twin Peaks?" Urshanabi asked.

"Yes," Gilgamesh nodded.

"What are the Twin Peaks? I've not heard of them before." Urshanabi looked puzzled. Gilgamesh cast a weary eye at him and sighed in frustration.

"The Twin Peaks are two huge mountains with peaks so high they reach the heavens. Their bases descend so far down they penetrate to the Deep. Between the two mountains lies a long, dark tunnel. Every night when the sun disappears from the horizon, it enters the mouth of this tunnel. It moves through the tunnel during the night until it reaches the other end. When it comes out at the other end, it lights up the sky, bringing daylight to mark the beginning of each new day."

"Huh," Urshanabi said. "I didn't know that."

"Well, where do you think the sun goes each night when it disappears from the sky, when the world is plunged into darkness?" Gilgamesh asked, his frustration obvious.

"I hadn't really given it much thought," Urshanabi replied. He opened his mouth to say more because he was still confused. But a stern look from Utnapishtim warned him to keep quiet. He snapped his mouth shut.

"When the sun sets, it enters the tunnel deep in the bowels of the earth between the two mountains," Gilgamesh repeated, sighing. He sensed Urshanabi still didn't understand. "It moves through the tunnel during the night. When it reaches the end of the tunnel, it surfaces through the opening, marking the beginning of a new day."

"Oh," Urshanabi sighed. "Now I understand," he said, although he really didn't. "But I'm just wondering . . ." Urshanabi began when Utnapishtim interrupted him mid-sentence.

"Get on with your story, son," he said to Gilgamesh as he stabbed Urshanabi with a piercing glare.

"It wasn't my first visit to these mountains," Gilgamesh said, looking sideways at Urshanabi. "I'd been there before, ages ago—long before I'd met Enkidu. I'd gone there alone, seeking an adventure. And I found one. It was late afternoon when I first heard them. I heard the roar long before I saw them. Their roar was loud and echoed throughout the valley. Lions. Huge lions. When they finally appeared on the horizon, I saw how big they were—bigger than any lions I'd ever seen. They were fearless. No animal could defeat them.

"I got scared. I prayed to Sin, the moon god, to protect me. But then I must have fallen asleep. When I woke up, I saw the lions had crept closer to me. I jumped up, ready to fight. Sin answered my prayers. He endowed me with the courage and strength to protect myself. I held my axe in one hand and my knife in the other. I charged at the lions. I smashed them to pieces."

Gilgamesh smiled recollecting how he had celebrated his triumph by proudly holding up the carcass of each lion on either side of him.

"I took the lions back to Uruk to show my people. They recorded my bravery by casting stone tablets of my image carrying a lion in each hand."

Gilgamesh bowed his head, his shoulders slumped. Those same feelings of triumph and victory had long since eluded him.

"I was a different person then," he said. "Much happier. So much has happened since then; so much has changed." His thoughts trailed off.

"That's all right, son," Old Woman said. "Go back to your story of how you came out here."

With a sudden jerk, Gilgamesh was jolted back to his present surroundings and the listeners who waited for him to resume his story.

"Where was I?"

"You set off heading east and then arrived at the Twin Peaks," Urshanabi prompted him.

"Oh, yes," Gilgamesh said, recalling his story. "There I was standing between the two mountains. I faced the black opening of the tunnel. I knew I had to get through the tunnel between those mountains to get to the Garden of the Gods. And from there, I could get to Utnapishtim. This time there were no lions to confront. But there was another problem."

"Oh?" Urshanabi asked. "Another problem? This is such an exciting adventure," he said.

The words leapt out of his mouth before he could snap it shut. Out of the corner of his eye, he could see Utnapishtim glaring at him. He fidgeted uncomfortably in his chair, lowering his eyes to avoid Utnapishtim's stare.

"The tunnel was protected by two guardians," Gilgamesh said. "They were half human, half dragon. Such fierce-looking monsters! They were known as the Scorpion People. Their job was to prevent anyone from entering the tunnel."

"You mean the same way that Humbaba had to prevent anyone from entering the Cedar Forest?" Old Woman asked.

Gilgamesh nodded. He felt a creeping discomfort at the mention of Humbaba's name. She just can't help it, he mumbled to himself. She just had to do it. She had to bring Humbaba up again.

"What did you do, son? Did you go after them and kill them the way you killed Humbaba? The way you killed the Bull of Heaven? That's the first thing that comes to your mind, isn't it?" She was persistent.

"No," Gilgamesh snapped. "It's not what comes to my mind every single time." Always with her relentless, tiresome line of questioning, he said to himself. Always reminding me.

"No, I didn't try to kill the Scorpion People. I didn't feel I should." He lowered his eyes and looked at his feet.

Old Woman and Utnapishtim exchanged meaningful glances. It occurred to them maybe the young man had learned something from his ordeal, after all. Maybe he'd learned not everything in front of him was an obstacle. Maybe he'd even learned not every apparent obstacle had to be confronted with an unprovoked act of violence.

"Why didn't you go after the Scorpion People?" Old Woman insisted, trying to draw an admission out of him. "Well, for one thing, I was alone. I didn't have Enkidu by my side to help me. And for another, the Scorpion People looked terrifying. They were half human, half dragon. They could cast the eye of death on you just by looking at you. I was scared of them. I had to shield my eyes from their glare. It took several minutes for my eyes to grow accustomed to their aura. I approached them cautiously. I thought I would try talking to them to see if they would help me."

Gilgamesh paused, taking several deep breaths.

"In other words, you decided to use your words instead of just charging forward, brandishing your weapons?"

Gilgamesh ignored her.

"The Scorpion Man called out to me. 'What's your name?' he shouted. 'Why have you made such a long journey? Why are you here?'

"He was gruff. His voice sent chills down my spine. He sounded angry. I could see he meant business. He demanded an answer.

"'No mortal has ever dared to travel as far as you've traveled. No one has crossed the seas, climbed the mountains, and trudged through deserts and wastelands to come this far. Why are you here?' he insisted.

"I had to tell him my story.

"My name is Gilgamesh, I said to him. I am King of Uruk. And then I told him all about Enkidu. I told him how much I loved him. I told him how he died. And I told him about my grief. I said I was on my way to find my ancestor, Utnapishtim the Faraway, the son of Ubara Tutu, to learn his story, to learn how he cheated death."

Gilgamesh bowed his head in silence and stared at the ground.

"So . . . what happened then?" Urshanabi asked with growing impatience. "Did you take out your axe and smash them?"

Gilgamesh ignored him.

"The Scorpion Man tried to dissuade me from going any further. He told me to go back home. He said no mortal had ever obtained the answers I sought. And no mortal had ever attempted to make it through the tunnel the sun travels during the night.

"'It's pitch black in there,' he said. 'There's no light at all. It gets darker and darker the deeper you go,' he warned me. 'If you don't make it to the other side before the sun enters the tunnel, you'll be burnt to a crisp. You'll never make it out in time.' He refused to open the gate to let me through. 'It's far too dangerous,' he said. 'I can't let you risk it.'

"I didn't know what to do. I had made it this far but now I was told I could go no further. The Scorpion Man had denied me access to the tunnel leading to the Garden of the Gods. I was baffled. I was stuck. I didn't want to go back. I couldn't go forward. That's when the Scorpion Woman spoke up. She spoke on my behalf. She convinced the Scorpion Man to change his mind.

"'Let him through,' she said to him. 'He's a brave man. He's gripped by despair for the loss of his brother. He's come such a long way. You've warned him of the dangers. You can do no more. He's still willing to take the risk. It's his decision to make. Let him through. Let him go so he can find Utnapishtim. Let him find the answers he seeks,' she pleaded."

"So . . ." interrupted Old Woman, eager to take advantage of the opportunity. "The Scorpion Woman showed you compassion. She felt sorry for you in your loss. She wanted to help you."

Gilgamesh nodded. He looked up at her, half-suspecting where she would take him.

"It's good to show compassion, isn't it?" she persisted. "It's good to feel for another in his grief, isn't it?" She raised her eyebrows inquisitively. A mischievous grin scrawled across her face.

Gilgamesh glared at her but didn't reply. Another one of her probing questions. He knew where she was going. She was trying to trick him into admitting something he didn't want to admit. She was reminding him of his killing of Humbaba. He didn't appreciate being reminded of the incident. He didn't like the way she jumped in at every opportunity to allude to it.

An awkward silence descended on the room. Urshanabi fidgeted. Old Woman and Gilgamesh locked eyes, neither side willing to be the first to blink. Finally, Utnapishtim broke the silence.

"Get on with your story, son," he said, frowning at his wife.

Gilgamesh intentionally turned his gaze away from the woman and focused his attention on Utnapishtim.

"The Scorpion Man was swayed by the Scorpion Woman's words. He opened the gates to the tunnel to let me go through. He cautioned me to run as fast as I could through its twelve leagues of darkness.

"'You must never stop,' he said. 'No matter how tired you get, you must run, run, and keep running. You have only twelve hours to get to the other side before the sun sets and enters the tunnel. You'll never survive the sun's raging fire if you don't get out in time.'

"I was terrified, but I had no choice. I had to go through with it even if it meant my death. I was determined to find you," he said, looking pointedly at Utnapishtim.

Gilgamesh gulped and took a deep breath.

"The Scorpion People were kind. They wished me peace. They wished me success on my journey. They gave me their blessing. They stepped aside to let me enter the tunnel. I saw the gaping darkness in front of me. I was afraid. I hesitated. But I couldn't turn back. I needed to find answers. I entered the black void at the tunnel's opening.

"The Scorpion Man was right. No sooner did I enter the tunnel than I was swallowed up in its darkness. It was pitch black in front of me, pitch black behind me, and pitch black on either side of me. I followed the Scorpion Man's advice. I began running as fast as I could. I ran deeper and deeper into the tunnel. I didn't think it was possible for it to get any darker. But the more I ran, the darker it got.

"I kept running and running. I must have run for what felt like several hours. I thought I would collapse from exhaustion. I despaired of ever reaching the end. Tears streamed down my face. Sweat poured from my body. My muscles ached. My legs stumbled. I forced them to push forward. I struggled to keep moving in spite of my exhaustion. I was scared. My body was in so much pain. I called out to the gods for help. Not one of them answered my prayer. I was alone. It was blacker than black all around. I had never felt more alone my whole life.

"I kept running and running. I thought I'll never make it out alive. I thought I'll never survive this. But then I felt a slight breeze on my face. It was still pitch black so I couldn't see anything. But the breeze gave me confidence I was nearing the end of the tunnel. I kept running, pushing forward with what little strength I had left. I was running to save my life. And then I saw it. In the distance ahead of me, I saw a glimmer of light. I ran toward it.

"And then I felt it. I felt hot air fanning my back and legs. I knew it was now or never. The sun was entering the tunnel at the other end. I forced myself to exert one final push. I scrambled out of the tunnel and tumbled into the light. I did it just as the sun entered its opening on the other end. I had escaped from the tunnel by the skin of my teeth. I had barely managed to make it out alive."

Gilgamesh paused and took a long, deep breath. His audience heaved a collective sigh and sat back in their chairs.

"Wow! That must have been something!" Urshanabi said, unable to conceal his excitement and admiration. "I don't think I could ever do anything like that," he said.

Gilgamesh scoffed and shrugged his shoulders, dismissing his feat as if it were nothing out of the ordinary. Utnapishtim sighed but didn't offer a comment or opinion. Old Woman stared in front of her, looking non-committal.

"What happened next?" Urshanabi asked. "Were you in the Garden of the Gods? What was it like? Tell us what it was like," he insisted. He was excited. He had never met a human who had walked through the Garden of the Gods before.

"Yes, I had arrived at the Garden of the Gods," Gilgamesh said. "At first, I couldn't look. It was so bright. Don't forget my eyes had seen nothing but darkness for twelve hours. It took me several minutes before I could accustom them to the light. But gradually I was able to open my eyes and see clearly. And what I saw took my breath away."

"Yes, yes," Urshanabi said, anxious to hear more. "Go on. Describe it to us. What was it like?"

"It was wonderful!" Gilgamesh said. "I'd never seen anything like it. Everything sparkled and glittered. Colorful gems were everywhere I looked. The garden was filled with trees. But these were no ordinary trees. These trees were covered with every stone imaginable—large stones of emerald, sapphire, agate, hematite, pearls, diamonds. Some of the branches leaned heavily with deep red rubies; some branches had flowers of lapis lazuli; and some branches hung clusters of gigantic coral. The bushes and vines dangled bunches of carnelians. Everywhere I looked I could see trees and sparkling gems. Everything dazzled the eyes. It was wonderful! I'd never seen anything like it," he repeated, sighing.

"Wow! That must have been something," Urshanabi said. "I would love to see it for myself some time."

"Why haven't you seen it?" Gilgamesh asked. "You must have seen it. You're right by it on the waterfront. All you have to do is walk a short distance and you'll be right there."

"But I am not allowed to go there," Urshanabi replied. "I can't even peek. The gods have ordered me to stay by the water. I'm to be ready to ferry Shamash across the waters whenever he wants. The Garden of the Gods is reserved strictly for them. Only they are allowed in there. They don't want any mortals wandering around."

"That's a fine time to remember obedience to the gods," Utnapishtim interrupted him. "If only you could remember to obey all the gods' commands and not just those that suit you."

He scowled at Urshanabi. No, I haven't forgotten what you did, he said with his eyes. I haven't forgotten how you disobeyed the gods by bringing a stranger to these shores.

"I guess that explains why Shamash was angry to see me there," Gilgamesh said, hurriedly. "But still, it's a pity you can't see it. The sight was breathtaking." He turned to Utnapishtim. "But you must have seen the Garden of the Gods before, haven't you?"

"No, we haven't," Utnapishtim replied.

"I don't understand," Gilgamesh said. "The gods granted you eternal life, didn't they? They made you like gods. They brought you to this island, didn't they? How did they get you here if you didn't pass through the Garden of the Gods?"

"The gods brought us here by a different route," Utnapishtim replied. "It's a long story, son. I'll tell it to you later. For now, why don't you finish telling us your story?"

"All right," Gilgamesh agreed. "But there's not much more to tell. I was walking around the Garden of the Gods, admiring its beauty, when I saw Shamash walking toward me. He was angry at seeing me there.

"'Why are you here?' he asked me. 'You're dressed in animal skins and you've eaten animal flesh. I can smell it on you. You shouldn't be here. You don't belong. No mortal has the right to be here.'

"I explained to Shamash why I had come. But my explanation didn't calm him any. He was still angry. And then he told me what I didn't want to hear. He told me I would never find the answers I sought. He told me to go back where I came from. I didn't want to believe him. I hadn't come all that way only to be told my journey was useless. I refused to accept it. I had to find a way. I remembered Enkidu's dream. I remembered the bird feathers. I couldn't face it. I had to discover the truth."

"How could you ignore Shamash's advice, son?" Utnapishtim asked. "Don't you know how dangerous that is?"

Gilgamesh shrugged. "I had no intention of giving up so easily. I walked and walked until I reached the edge of the sea. It was there I found Siduri."

Old Woman sat up with a jerk. "Siduri? You found Siduri? You found the winemaker of the gods?"

Gilgamesh was startled by Old Woman's sudden interest in someone so unexceptional.

"Yes," he said. "Why? What's so special about Siduri?"

"You don't know?" She was surprised he hadn't heard of Siduri.

"I know she's the wine maker of the gods, if that's what you're asking. I don't know why you're so excited about Siduri. I didn't think there was anything special about her at all."

Old Woman shook her head in disbelief.

Chapter 15: The Wine Maker

"You don't understand, son" she said. "Siduri is not just the wine maker of the gods. She is a wise woman. I would love to meet her and learn from her. Did you talk to her? Did she say anything to you? Did she give you any advice? Did you listen to her?"

"Yes, we talked," Gilgamesh said with a shrug. "But I wasn't impressed. She was sitting in her garden when I first saw her. She was making wine in a large golden bowl. She must have seen me coming. She ran inside her tavern, bolted the door, and ran up to her roof. She watched me from a safe distance. I can't say I blame her for being afraid of me. I probably looked a scary mess."

"What did you do?"

"Well, I wasn't going to put up with her locking me out," Gilgamesh replied, a sharp brusqueness in his voice. "I went up to the tavern and thumped my fist as loud as I could on the door. I threatened her. I said I would break her door down. I would force my way in if she didn't open it. I meant it. And to prove I was capable of doing what I said, I told her my name. I said I am Gilgamesh of Uruk. I killed Humbaba of the Cedar Forest. I killed the Bull of Heaven. I killed the lions near the mountain pass."

"You threatened her?" You threatened Siduri? How could you do that? Have you no respect?" Old Woman said, her agitation palpable.

"Respect? Respect for her? What's there to respect? All she does is make wine for the gods. I wasn't afraid of her. And, yes, I threatened her," Gilgamesh said. He puffed out his chest. He looked at Old Woman defiantly.

"But it didn't do any good. At first, she didn't believe me. She asked me for an explanation. 'If you really are who you say you are, why do you look so miserable?

GILGAMESH OF URUK

The Gilgamesh who killed Humbaba, who killed the Bull of Heaven, who killed the lions of the mountain pass is strong and powerful. He is a great king. You don't look anything like a great king to me. You look thin and weary and sad. You look like a child who has lost his way.'

"I had to explain my story. I had to tell her who I was and why I was there. She came down from the roof and slowly unbolted the door. I noticed her bony fingers first. They were colored a dark red—probably from making the wine. And then her eyes. They were black and piercing. Her stare was intense, penetrating. I had to look away. I felt she could see through me.

"'What do you want, Gilgamesh?' she said.

"I told her I needed her help. I told her I wanted to know the secret of eternal life. I told her I didn't want to die. I told her about my beloved Enkidu. I asked her to help me get eternal life." He looked expectantly at Old Woman.

"She can't do that," she said. "She can't give you eternal life. You should have known better than to ask her for that. What did she say to you?"

"She laughed at me," Gilgamesh said.

"Well, that doesn't surprise me."

Old Woman sat back in her chair, pleased with Siduri's reaction. It serves the boy right, she thought. Siduri's reputation for wisdom was well-deserved.

"She must have thought I was joking," Gilgamesh said.

He shot a piercing glance in the direction of the old woman. She met his glare with a mocking smile.

"But when she realized I was serious, she became serious. She told me the same thing Shamash had told me—that I would never find what I was seeking. She said when the gods created humans, they withheld from them the gift of immortality. They reserved eternal life for themselves. 'It's the fate of humans to be born, to live, and to die,' she told me. 'There's nothing you can do to change that.'"

"I told you the same thing down by the water," Utnapishtim interjected, his frustration evident. "Don't you remember?"

"Is that all she said?" Old Woman asked, ignoring Utnapishtim.

"No. She gave me some choice words of wisdom," Gilgamesh said, his voice laced with sarcasm. "'Go home,' she said. 'Love your child. Give pleasure to your wife. Surround yourself with beautiful things. Eat well. Bathe and anoint your body with soothing oils. Wear colorful garments. Celebrate with music. Dance. Enjoy your life. Let happiness enter your heart, for this, too, is the lot of man.'"

Gilgamesh rattled off the words with a sneer.

"That's good advice. You should consider it." Old Woman nodded her head encouragingly.

"How can I?" Gilgamesh asked, his voice sounding increasingly agitated. "How can I take her advice? How can I forget my Enkidu is dust and my fate is to become dust? How can I go on living knowing I'm to die? What kind of advice is that to give to a person suffering from a great loss?"

"Son, did you even try to understand Siduri's advice?"

"No, I didn't need to," Gilgamesh replied curtly. He glared at her. "She gave me the same advice I've heard a hundred times over, the same advice everyone else has given me. Including my mother. Including Utnapishtim. She didn't tell me anything I haven't heard before."

"Let me explain it to you, son. It's possible you didn't understand."

Old Woman glanced at Utnapishtim and shook her head. This boy is such a fool, she said with her eyes. He

GILGAMESH OF URUK

nodded. Out of the corner of her eye, she saw Gilgamesh rolling his eyes in frustration. She ignored his signs of irritation. The boy must be made to understand.

"First of all, Siduri wanted to know who you are and why you look so grief-stricken. She wanted to understand you to give you the best advice."

Gilgamesh sighed and folded his arms. He made no attempt to disguise his weariness.

"Siduri advised you to accept your mortality. That's good advice, son. No matter how hard you fight against it, you'll not be able to change it. Accept it, son. Learn to live with the knowledge you'll die. You're a warrior. You should know better than anyone it's useless to fight a battle when the outcome has already been determined. Why take on a battle you know you'll lose? Accept your fate. It's the fate of all mankind. Move on. That's good advice.

"Siduri also advised you to appreciate what you have. She urged you to love those you have in your life. She advised you to start a family. She told you to love your future child, to give pleasure to your future wife. Be thankful you can have a family. Embrace them when they enter your life."

"That's the same advice mother always gives me," Gilgamesh interrupted her. "'Settle down, son,' she says to me. 'Take a wife, have children.' But I don't have a wife. I don't have children. The only person I ever loved is Enkidu. Now Enkidu is gone."

"You will have a wife. You will have children one day," Old Woman assured him. "But think about it, son. In some ways, you already have a wife and children. You're king of Uruk. Your family means more than just a spouse and child. It also means the people of your kingdom. They're your family. You're the head of that family. Siduri's advice means embrace your subjects, understand their needs, help them to find happiness.

You'll find peace when you focus on the needs of others. Don't just focus on yourself, on your needs."

She paused to take a deep breath. She hoped her words registered.

"Siduri also told you to remember you have a responsibility to yourself. She reminded you to bathe, to anoint your body, to wear colorful clothes. Believe me, son, looking good and feeling good about your appearance will improve your mental state. A healthy body leads to a healthy mind.

"And, lastly, Siduri advised you to dance, to celebrate, to live your life to the fullest, to live in joy and happiness."

"That's easy to say but not so easy to do," Gilgamesh retorted.

"Listen to me, son. Once you accept your fate is to die, you'll have a choice to make. Do you want to spend the rest of your life whining and wallowing in self-pity? Or do you want to spend it by leading a responsible life? You're a king. You should lead by example. Give joy to others. Seek enjoyment in your own life. Embrace all life has to offer. The choice is yours to make."

Old Woman paused to allow him time to reflect on her words.

"Make the right choice, son," she urged him. "Take Siduri's advice. Follow the path she recommended."

Gilgamesh sighed.

"You're not telling me anything I haven't heard before," he said dismissively. "What you're not telling me, what anyone has yet to tell me is how? How am I supposed to live a life full of joy? How can I celebrate what I have when I'm miserable? How can I be happy when I know I must die? How can I be happy when I have lost Enkidu? Am I supposed to just snap my fingers and suddenly feel better? I'm telling you my heart is broken. You're telling me to bathe and wear colorful clothes and dance. How? How can I do this?"

"Son, listen to me. Suffering is a part of life. Joy and beauty are also a part of life. They're all woven together. You can't untangle them. You've experienced intense sorrow. That opens you up to feel for the sorrow of others. It also opens you up to experience the intense joy of life. Embrace both the sorrow and the joy and you will find peace."

Gilgamesh stared at her, a bewildered expression on his face. But she wasn't ready to give up.

"Knowing you'll one day die should make you want to make the most of the time you have. That's the wisdom of Siduri. Live life to the fullest. Eat well. Sleep well. Love those around you. They may not be around you for very long. You may not be around for very long. Be good to others. Be good to yourself. You don't know when your life will be snuffed out, when the gods will fasten the eye of death on you. Meanwhile, embrace life in all its disappointments and pain, in all its beauty and joy."

Old Woman leaned back in her chair. She folded her arms. She had nothing more to add.

Gilgamesh still looked skeptical. "But you're not telling me how to do that," he complained. "How can I embrace the joy in life when all I see is pain and suffering, decay and death?"

"Look for the beauty in life and you'll find it."

She lowered her eyes. She didn't have any more answers for him. Nothing more she could say would satisfy him while he was in his current frame of mind. She had shown him the path. But she couldn't force him to take it. He had to follow the path himself when he was ready. She sighed. She hoped in time he would recognize the wisdom in Siduri's advice and heal himself.

Gilgamesh waited for her to speak, but she had nothing more to add.

"As I was saying before I was interrupted, Siduri wasn't much help," he continued. He locked his eyes on the old woman.

"When I realized Siduri couldn't provide me with answers, I asked her for directions to Utnapishtim. She tried to dissuade me from finding you," he said, turning to Utnapishtim. "She said it was impossible for any mortal to cross the ocean to get to you. Only Shamash could do that. She warned me about the Waters of Death. She said that if even a drop of those waters touched me, I would die instantly.

"I refused to give up. I persisted. I told her I could take care of myself. I asked her for directions. Finally, she told me about Urshanabi, your ferryman. She told me where I could find him on the water's edge. She said he was in the forest with the Stone Men. She said he might agree to take me across. Otherwise, I would have no choice but to go back where I came from. I ignored her warning. I went to the water's edge to look for Urshanabi."

Upon hearing his name, Urshanabi perked up. He knew the rest of the story. He wanted to present his version to vindicate himself with Utnapishtim.

"Yes, yes," he said, eager to interject his voice. "That's how we met. That's when I first saw Gilgamesh."

"What happened then?" Utnapishtim asked.

"Well, I told Urshanabi I wanted his help to cross the Waters of Death to get to you," Gilgamesh replied.

"No, no. Wait a minute," Urshanabi interrupted him. "That's not exactly how it happened."

Gilgamesh fidgeted uncomfortably in his chair. He lowered his eyes to avoid looking at his listeners.

"What do you mean? What happened?" Utnapishtim asked.

Urshanabi looked inquiringly at Gilgamesh.

"Urshanabi, tell me what happened." Utnapishtim's voice was firm.

Urshanabi hesitated, not knowing whether he should tell the story or allow Gilgamesh to speak. He glanced at Gilgamesh who had buried his face in his hands.

"What happened?" Utnapishtim demanded. He looked sternly at Urshanabi.

"He killed them," Urshanabi replied. He looked downcast, speaking barely above a whisper.

"Killed who? Whom did he kill?" Utnapishtim asked. "What are you talking about?" He leaned forward attentively in his seat.

"He killed the Stone Men. He killed the Stone Men who ferry us across the Waters of Death," Urshanabi replied. "He killed them before I could stop him."

Old Woman gasped.

"What? He did what . . .? Killed the Stone Men?" Utnapishtim's voice shook. "I don't believe it. He killed the Stone Men? The Stone Men are dead?"

Utnapishtim looked at Old Woman, horrified.

"Gilgamesh, you killed the Stone Men? Why? Why?" He fixed his eyes sternly at Gilgamesh.

"Answer me. This makes no sense. The Stone Men can cross the Waters of Death unscathed. I don't understand. Why did you do it?"

Gilgamesh kept his head bowed and his eyes lowered.

"I don't know," he muttered, shrugging his shoulders. "I don't know why I did it. But what he says is true. I killed the Stone Men. I killed them all."

Chapter 16: The Ferryman

Utnapishtim and Old Woman gasped. It took them several minutes to digest the information. They couldn't understand it. Why would you kill the very creatures who could help you get to your destination without risk? They stared at each other, searching for answers. The tension in the air was palpable. The lengthy silence following Gilgamesh's admission finally broke with Old Woman.

"Why did you kill them, son?" she asked, her voice subdued and barely audible.

Questions about Gilgamesh and his propensity for violence whirled in her mind. Why did he have such a compulsion to kill? Why attack when he wasn't provoked? Surely his encounter with the Scorpion People had shown he was capable of resisting the urge to kill? So why did his impulse to kill resurface? Why kill the Stone Men before even giving them the opportunity to help him? She was baffled by his behavior.

Gilgamesh didn't immediately respond to her question. She waited before asking it again.

"Son, I asked you a question. Why did you kill the Stone Men?"

"I don't know," Gilgamesh mumbled under his breath. He looked bewildered and shook his head. "I was tired," he offered by way of explanation. "I had come such a long way. I had overcome so many obstacles. I was so close. Everyone—from the Scorpion People to Shamash to Siduri—everyone was telling me to turn back. They said I'd fail. I was angry. I was frustrated. I wanted to lash out at someone, at something."

"Yes, but . . ." she interrupted him.

"I went looking for the Stone Men. I wanted to force them to obey me. For one thing, Siduri had made it clear

GILGAMESH OF URUK

they were my last hope. I guess I wanted to prove my strength to them, to scare them into doing as I asked. I wasn't going to let them dismiss me the way everyone else had. But when I finally found them, I guess I must have . . . I guess I sort of lost control. I went a bit crazy. I attacked them without really thinking."

Gilgamesh shook his head, frowning. "I killed them. I killed them all," he repeated. He raised his head and looked at Urshanabi. "I even threatened to kill him if he refused to ferry me across," he added, nodding at Urshanabi.

"That's right," Urshanabi said, anxious to describe his version of the events. "He's telling the truth. He threatened to kill me if I didn't help him. I had no choice." Urshanabi looked imploringly at Utnapishtim. He hoped for understanding. He craved his master's forgiveness.

"I found them in the forest, just as Siduri had said," Gilgamesh continued. "I sneaked up on them quietly. I had my axe in one hand and my knife in the other. I had intended to shout, to scare them. I crept up close and screamed out my battle cry. But then something in me must have snapped. The next thing I knew, I had pounced on them. Before I could stop myself, before I even knew what I was doing, I was smashing them into little pieces. I lost control. I couldn't stop myself. All my pent-up rage, all my frustration and disappointment took control of me. I lashed out. I didn't stop to think what I was doing. I crushed them into little pieces."

Old Woman let out another gasp. "But . . . but why?" She stammered her words. "I don't understand. Why such brutality? Why didn't you stop to think they might help you? Didn't you learn something from your encounter with the Scorpion People? They helped you, didn't they? Siduri helped you, didn't she? Why didn't you just ask the Stone Men for help? I don't understand," she repeated. "It makes no sense. Why did you do it, son? Why did you kill them?"

"I smashed them into little pieces. I threw them into the sea. I watched them sink," Gilgamesh said. He squirmed in his chair. He lowered his gaze, staring intently at the ground to avoid eye contact.

Old Woman sank back in her chair. She was speechless. Utnapishtim was also at a loss for words. He grunted and shook his head in dismay. Urshanabi decided the ensuing lull in the conversation was his opportunity to present his version of the events. He seized his chance. He jumped in before anyone else spoke up.

"It was a day that started out like any other," Urshanabi began. He settled himself back comfortably in his chair, eager to spin his yarn. "I was out with the Stone Men trimming branches like we usually do. Suddenly, I heard this shout. I turned around. Before I knew what was happening, I saw him charging straight at the Stone Men," he said, nodding at Gilgamesh. "I didn't have time to stop him or do anything. He just went after them. He was like a crazy man. He smashed them to pieces. He yelled and screamed the whole time. I didn't know what was happening. And those poor Stone Men. They didn't know what hit them. They didn't even have a chance to defend themselves.

"Gilgamesh attacked them with a fury. He chopped them up. He tossed their broken bits and pieces into the sea. He stood in front of me, brandishing his knife and axe. He defied me to challenge him. I could tell he was itching for another fight. He wasn't satisfied with just killing the Stone Men. He waited for me to make the smallest move. He wanted an excuse to pounce on me just as he did the Stone Men. I was scared. I thought he was going to kill me for sure."

Urshanabi paused briefly. He wanted Utnapishtim to understand. He had been scared for his life. He had had no choice.

"I really thought he was going to kill me," he repeated, his eyes pleading with Utnapishtim. "I knew I was no match for his strength. I thought I was going to die for sure. But instead of attacking me, Gilgamesh just stood there, staring into open space. His arms went limp. His weapons dangled loosely by his side. He got a sort of glazed look in his eyes. He looked like a broken man. Not at all like the fierce, angry warrior who had just killed the Stone Men.

"I didn't know what to do. I was afraid to move in case he thought I was trying to attack him. I decided to talk to him to calm him down. I introduced myself. And then I asked him his name. 'My name is Gilgamesh and I am king of Uruk.'" Urshanabi puffed up his chest to mimic Gilgamesh's mannerisms.

Sitting further back in his chair, Urshanabi paused briefly. He had gained the rapt interest of his listeners. He relished their undivided attention, unaccustomed as he was to being at the center of any conversation. He enjoyed the novelty, intending to sustain it for as long as he could. He dragged out his story.

"Gilgamesh began telling me of his long journey through mountains and valleys and deserts," he said, resuming his tale. "He claimed to have overcome many hazards to get here. He even claimed to have traveled through the Deep. I wasn't sure I believed him, at least the part about him traveling to the Deep. I had heard stories of mortals traveling there. I'd even heard some of them had come out unharmed. But I didn't really believe any of them. I thought they were silly rumors. I doubted it was even possible to make the journey to the Deep as a living mortal. But I decided not to quibble with Gilgamesh. I just listened. And then he told me he had made this long journey with one purpose in mind—to find you, Master," he said looking at Utnapishtim. "And he asked for my help."

"But he had killed the Stone Men," Utnapishtim interrupted him. "They're the only ones who can ferry you safely across the Waters of Death. How were you able to bring him here without them?"

"Well, it wasn't easy," Urshanabi said. "First of all, I had to break the news to him he had made it much harder for us to cross the Waters of Death without the Stone Men. I was afraid he would lash out at me when he heard the news. But he just stood there, staring into space, his eyes empty. By now his whole manner had changed. He looked bewildered and helpless, not at all like the crazy man who had just butchered the Stone Men. I guess I must have felt sorry for him. I don't know. Maybe I was just scared of him. Anyway, I told him what he needed to do."

"Get to the point, Urshanabi," Utnapishtim interrupted him, this time with increasing impatience. He fixed his stare on Urshanabi and began strumming his fingers on the nearby table in frustration.

"I am only interested in learning how you crossed the Waters of Death without the Stone Men," he repeated. "There's no need for a lengthy overture. Just get us to the Waters of Death."

Old Woman glanced at Utnapishtim. She fidgeted nervously in her chair.

"Be patient with me, Master. I'm getting there," Urshanabi said. "As I was saying, I told Gilgamesh to cut down poles for punting. I estimated we needed three hundred, each about one hundred feet long. He was to strip them of their bark and to fashion grips on them for easy holding.

"Gilgamesh finished the task quickly. Together we placed the poles on the boat and sailed out on the ocean.

We didn't stop to rest. We worked well together, taking it in turns to rest and steer the boat."

"Yes, yes," Utnapishtim said, showing his annoyance at Urshanabi. The strumming on the table got progressively louder. "I'm sure it was all very wonderful. I'm not interested in hearing about how you collaborated to cross the ocean or what a jolly time you had doing it or how you bonded with each other. I want to know what happened when you got to the Waters of Death. How did you cross the Waters without the Stone Men?"

"If you give me a chance, I'll explain, Master," Urshanabi replied. "But I can't do it if you keep interrupting me."

"Well, get on with it," Utnapishtim shouted from across the room.

"Husband, be patient," Old Woman intervened. "Let the man speak. The more you interrupt him, the longer it will take for him to tell us his story."

She was visibly agitated, anticipating the inevitable.

Utnapishtim grunted. His eyes stabbed Urshanabi with a menacing look that made Urshanabi fidget uncomfortably in his chair.

"Go on, Urshanabi," she said, reassuringly. "Finish your story. The quicker you get this over with, the better it'll be for all of us."

"We sailed across the ocean without stopping," Urshanabi continued, focusing his eyes on the woman. "It normally takes six weeks of sailing to get to the Waters of Death, but it took us only three days. Can you believe it? Only three days! As I said, we worked well together and took turns to rest."

"Urshanabi, if you don't get to the point right now, I will make you regret it," Utnapishtim interrupted him again, his face red, his eyes flashing, and his fist banging on the nearby table. "You got to the Waters of Death. What happened next?"

One look at Utnapishtim and Urshanabi knew his master had reached the end of his patience. He sensed it would not be in his best interest to prolong the story any further. He quickened the pace.

"After three days of sailing," he said, rushing to speak, "we finally reached the Waters of Death."

Utnapishtim sat up and leaned forward. The strumming stopped.

"I told Gilgamesh to take the poles one at a time and plunge each pole into the water to push us forward. I warned him to release the pole into the water as soon as his hands reached the top. He was to avoid letting even a drop of the Waters of Death touch any part of his body. Then he had to pick up the next pole and repeat the process. He was to do it the same way over and over until all three hundred poles had been used.

"As you know . . ." Urshanabi paused and inclined his head toward Old Woman to show he understood the perilous nature of the journey. "As you know," he repeated, puffing up his chest, "only the Stone Men could touch the Waters of Death and remain alive. The rest of us would die on the spot."

Utnapishtim sighed, folded his arms, and scowled. This prompted Urshanabi to finish his story.

"By maneuvering the boat and pushing it forward with the three hundred poles, we managed to get safely through the Waters of Death. But we hadn't quite made it to the shore yet. Gilgamesh picked up my robe and held it up in his hands like a sail. The wind pushed us forward. We finally made it to the shore of your island. So here we are, all in one piece, unscathed by the Waters of Death."

Urshanabi leaned back, grinning with pride. He was thrilled with the success of his plan. After all, it was quite a magnificent feat. No mortal had ever before been able to cross the Waters of Death without the Stone Men. And he, Urshanabi, the lowly servant of Utnapishtim, had shown it could be done. He was convinced his master's anger would dissipate now he had heard his version of the story.

Urshanabi even went so far as to anticipate words of approval from his master for having accomplished the impossible. Words like 'brilliant' and 'genius' came to his mind. An image flitted through his mind's eye of Utnapishtim tussling his hair in a friendly manner and patting him on the back to gesture all was forgiven.

But one glance at Utnapishtim told him his master was far from pleased. He looked angry, his eyes fixating on Urshanabi with an intense glare. He said nothing.

Old Woman fidgeted uncomfortably in her chair. She sensed the inevitable.

Urshanabi wiped the triumphant smile from his face sensing something was not quite right.

"That's how we did it, Master," he said, still hoping some words of praise might yet come tumbling out of Utnapishtim's mouth.

"So, that's how you did it," Utnapishtim said, a fierce expression on his face.

"Yes," Urshanabi replied. His voice faltered. He recognized the expression. He had seen it before. It made him feel uneasy. He lowered his eyes, afraid. He knew the look of anger on Utnapishtim's face. He held his breath, bracing himself anxiously for the inevitable eruption.

Chapter 17: The Apology

She wasn't surprised. She knew he would be angry. She knew a confrontation was inevitable. She was right.

Utnapishtim took a deep breath and followed it with another. He stood up slowly, staring hard at Urshanabi. He leaned on his cane and began tapping it on the floor. He barked out a barrage of questions.

"Let me ask you something, Urshanabi," he began. "Did it ever occur to you that when you showed Gilgamesh how to cross the Waters of Death without the Stone Men, you violated a trust? Did it occur to you the gods put Wife and I on this island surrounded by the Waters of Death for one reason and one reason alone—because they didn't want other mortals to have access to this island?"

"Master, I . . ." Urshanabi stuttered.

"Did it occur to you what you did was to reveal a secret the gods did not want revealed?"

Utnapishtim spoke through clenched teeth.

"Did it occur to you by violating the command of the gods you would get us all into trouble? Did it occur to you Gilgamesh might share this secret with others? Did it occur to you we might get a throng of visitors on this island because you don't know how to keep your stupid mouth shut? I ask you, Urshanabi, did any of this occur to you?"

Utnapishtim's voice had become louder with each successive question. By the time he reached the final question, he was yelling. He banged his cane on the floor, his eyes ablaze, his face red.

Urshanabi was stunned. His eyes caught the eyes of the old woman, pleading for help. He sank deep into his chair. He flustered and floundered, not knowing how to respond. It was obvious none of this had occurred to him. His hands shook. He cringed, afraid of angering

Utnapishtim, afraid of angering the gods. His lips moved as he tried to utter words. Nothing came out.

Utnapishtim wasn't done with him yet.

"I asked you a question, Urshanabi," he shouted, his face dark with rage. "Did any of this occur to you?"

"No," mumbled a terrified Urshanabi. He sank deeper into his chair.

"What?" Utnapishtim screamed at him, this time banging his fists on the table. "What did you say? Speak up. I didn't hear what you said."

"Utnapishtim, calm down," Old Woman said to reduce the tension.

"Wife, he needs to answer me! He must be made to understand. I ask you again, Urshanabi. Did any of this occur to you?"

"No, none of this occurred to me, Master," Urshanabi replied. He forced the words out with difficulty.

"I didn't think so. Don't you see what you've done? Don't you see the damage you caused, you fool?"

"Yes . . . but Master . . . he threatened to . . . to kill me if I didn't bring him to you," Urshanabi said, his voice feeble and shaking.

"I don't care what he threatened," Utnapishtim screamed. The fist thumping became louder. "You should have known better than to bring him here. You revealed a secret making it possible for others to cross the Waters of Death. You defied the gods. Do you understand what you've done? Do you understand how serious this is?"

"But . . . but . . . Master, I had no choice," Urshanabi pleaded. "He had already killed the Stone Men. And he insisted I help him get to you. What could I do? He would have killed me had I refused."

"Husband, calm down," Old Woman intervened. "There's no point getting upset about it now. What's done is done."

Utnapishtim's face burned red, his veins throbbed.

"What?" Utnapishtim spluttered. He turned to look at her. "What's that you say? Don't you see? The stupid fool has ruined everything. And he doesn't even realize it. He brags about what he's done. He drags out his story thinking he deserves our praise."

Utnapishtim turned to face Urshanabi, his eyes glaring. "The gods will punish you for this, mark my words."

"But, Master, it wasn't my fault," came Urshanabi's plaintive cry. "He threatened to kill me if I didn't help him."

"He's right," Gilgamesh said, speaking for the first time. "He didn't have a choice. Don't blame Urshanabi. It wasn't his fault. I would have killed him if he hadn't helped me."

"Don't try to defend his actions," Utnapishtim roared dismissively. "He had no business bringing you here. Now that you know it's possible to cross the Waters of Death without the Stone Men, who knows how often you'll be back? Who knows how many will try to make it out here when they learn the secret of how you did it? The island will be crawling with people before long. And then the gods will show their anger by punishing us all. No thanks to you."

Utnapishtim sat down in his chair, breathing heavily.

"You don't understand," he said, looking at Gilgamesh, his voice calmer. "This is a serious matter, son. The gods put Old Woman and I on this island after the deluge. They surrounded the island with the Waters of Death. They did it to prohibit any mortal foolish enough to try to make it here. Only the Stone Men could cross the Waters without fear. But now, thanks to this fool sitting there," he said, pointing at Urshanabi, "that's no longer the case. He's shown you how it can be done. Others are bound to follow."

"I'm sorry, Master," Urshanabi said. His hands trembled, his voice faltered.

"Tell that to the gods," Utnapishtim snarled, dismissing the apology with anger.

No one dared speak. The air was fraught with tension. Old Woman felt the need to speak up. She had listened to Urshanabi spin his tale. She had seen Utnapishtim's face burn with rage.

"Now, now, husband. It can't be as bad as all that."

"What do you mean?" Utnapishtim snapped. "You know as well as I do why the gods put us on this island. They saved us from the deluge. We were to live here alone. We were to have no visitors other than Shamash, Urshanabi, and the Stone Men. Do you think the gods will be pleased when they know the Waters of Death can be crossed without the Stone Men?"

"No, I don't think they'll be pleased. But I don't think this knowledge is going to do anyone any good," she added, trying to calm the situation.

"What? What do you mean?"

"Listen to me, husband. Calm down and think about it. You heard Gilgamesh describe the hardships he encountered in just getting to the Garden of the Gods. You heard him describe how he had to run through the dark tunnel of the Deep for twelve continuous hours to avoid being burnt to a crisp by the sun. Do you think that's an easy feat for a mortal? Do you think anyone else could successfully do what he did?"

"She's right," Gilgamesh chimed in, nodding his head eagerly. "There's only one other person I know with the strength and perseverance to make it as far as I have. That's my beloved Enkidu. And Enkidu is dead. No other mortal can endure the journey. I'm certain anyone else would die long before making it to the Garden of the Gods."

"What are you saying?" Utnapishtim asked.

"I'm saying even if I were to tell people of my journey, of how I made it this far, of how I crossed the Waters of Death, they wouldn't be able to use that knowledge. The journey is too dangerous. No mortal will risk his life by doing what I've done."

Urshanabi nodded.

"He's right, Master. No one else can make it this far. Only Gilgamesh is capable of doing it. Only Gilgamesh is strong enough and brave enough."

Utnapishtim shot a fierce glare at Urshanabi to silence him.

"But what about the gods?" he grunted.

"What about them?" Old Woman said.

"They're not going to be happy when they learn of this."

"No, they're not," she agreed. "But there's nothing we can do about that now. And since the chance of someone else performing Gilgamesh's feat is highly unlikely, it really doesn't matter, does it? What's done is done, Utnapishtim. There's no undoing it. And besides, Urshanabi knows better now than to bring anyone else to this island without your permission. Isn't that right, Urshanabi?"

"Yes," Urshanabi replied, his head bobbing up and down. "I'll never bring anyone else to this island without your permission, Master. I promise. Even if I'm threatened with death, I'll never again ferry anyone here unless I've cleared it with you first. I'm truly sorry, Master, for what I've done. It'll never happen again."

The foolish man opened his mouth to say more. But Old Woman didn't trust he would say the right thing. She frowned at him. She put her finger to her lips, cautioning him to stop babbling. He snapped his mouth shut and lowered his eyes.

Utnapishtim remained deep in thought for a few minutes. Finally, he spoke up.

"I don't know about this," he grumbled. "I don't like this turn of events at all. I'm not happy."

Gilgamesh tried to make amends.

"I'm so sorry," he began. "This is all my fault. I don't know why I did it. I don't know why I killed the Stone Men. I wasn't thinking. I was so tired and worn out. I was just so desperate to get to you."

Utnapishtim shook his head in disappointment.

"You don't understand, son. The gods went to great lengths to save Wife and I from the deluge. We were the only survivors granted eternal life. Everyone else who survived on the boat with us lived normal lives. They died at the time appointed for their deaths by the gods. The gods separated Old Woman and I from the rest of mankind. They gave us eternal life. They placed us on this island surrounded by the Waters of Death so others couldn't reach it. But now the secret is out. Anyone will be able to come."

"But that's not true," Gilgamesh interrupted him. "That's what I'm saying. It's too difficult a journey to get even this far. When I get back to Uruk, I'll tell the people of the hardships I experienced. I'll tell them of the hazards along the way. I'll tell them about having to run for twelve continuous hours in the tunnel of the Deep. I'll tell them I could have been burned by the sun if I didn't make it out in time. And I'll tell them about the Waters of Death, of how contact with even a drop will kill a person. No one will dare to make the same journey. The people know they'll die if they even try it.

"Remember, I am the strongest of mortals in Uruk," Gilgamesh said with a flourish. "I killed Humbaba. I killed the Bull of Heaven. Everyone knows of my legendary strength. No one alive can compete with me when it comes to bravery and strength and courage. You have nothing to worry about, Utnapishtim. No one else will risk making this journey. Believe me."

Utnapishtim remained silent.

Gilgamesh sought Old Woman's eyes for guidance. She nodded approvingly and smiled. She turned to Utnapishtim.

"Utnapishtim, husband," she said, softening her voice. "This young man has come all this way to hear about the deluge. He wants to know our story. He wants to know how we escaped from drowning when everyone else in our city died. He told us his story. Now it's our turn to tell him our story. It's his turn to listen. Why don't you tell him our story?"

Old Woman looked at Gilgamesh. She nodded her head, encouraging him to speak.

"Yes, yes," Gilgamesh replied, eager to take her cue. "I want to know what happened. I want to know how the gods granted you eternal life. Utnapishtim, please tell me your story. I've come all this way to hear it. Tell me. How did you manage to escape the flood? How did you cheat death?"

Utnapishtim shook his head, hesitating.

"It happened a very long time ago, son. I'm not sure I can even remember all the details."

"That's all right. Tell me what you can remember. I am anxious to hear it."

"Yes, Master, please tell it," Urshanabi said, eager to add his voice to the chorus of support. "It's such a wonderful story. I never get tired of hearing it."

Old Woman smiled. She knew Utnapishtim was perfectly capable of remembering all the details. She knew those fateful events were etched indelibly in his mind as they were in hers. After all, how could one forget such an experience? They had discussed it at length so many times. They had recollected the sequence of events so many times. He was just being coy, she thought. She knew it was good for him to talk about the flood even though it brought back painful memories for

GILGAMESH OF URUK

the two of them. And now he had an eager audience in the young man. He will lose himself in the story telling, she thought. He will forget all about his anger at Urshanabi. Maybe.

She caught Utnapishtim's eyes and smiled encouragingly.

"Go on, Utnapishtim. Tell the young man about the deluge. Tell him about the quarrel between the gods. Tell him about the pact the gods made with mortals. I know it brings back painful memories. But it's not as if the images or the sounds are far from our thoughts for any length of time, anyway. And, besides, this young man has come all this way to hear our story. Don't disappoint him, Utnapishtim. Tell him our story."

"The gods quarreled among themselves?" Gilgamesh asked to prompt Utnapishtim.

"Yes, son," Old Woman replied.

"Utnapishtim, the young man has come all this way," she repeated, pleading with her eyes. "Tell him our story of how we survived the flood."

Utnapishtim shrugged his shoulders. He took a deep breath and began his tale.

Chapter 18: The Flood

"It happened a long, long time ago," Utnapishtim sighed. "What do you know about our story, son?" he asked Gilgamesh.

"Not much," Gilgamesh replied. "I only know the little the elders have shared with us. They said there was some kind of flood and, somehow, you managed to get the gods to grant you immortality. You were able to cheat death. But the elders didn't know any of the details. That's why I'm here. I want to know how it happened."

"Have you heard of a city called Shuruppak?" Utnapishtim asked.

"Yes, I have. But I don't know anything about it other than the elders told us you came from there. I've never been there."

"Well, that doesn't surprise me. There's nothing of it left. It was an ancient city that lay along the Euphrates. And it was beautiful. Old Woman and I were born there and lived there most of our lives. I was proud to be the king of such a magnificent city."

"There was no place like it," Old Woman interrupted him.

She smiled, remembering.

"The city, the market place, the people, and the dwellings—it was all very beautiful in the early days. We had many friends and neighbors. We knew almost everyone in the city. People were friendly and kind. Neighbors helped each other out in times of need. It was a happy city, full of love, full of life.

"We tried to do everything right," she continued. "We celebrated the holy days and festivals. We honored the gods. We performed animal sacrifices for them. But we also knew how to enjoy life. Utnapishtim and I would sit under the shade trees in the gardens during the day, smelling the sweet fragrance of the flowers."

She turned to Utnapishtim. "Do you remember that? Do you remember how beautiful it was?"

Utnapishtim nodded.

"And in the evenings, we would watch the moon god, Sin, make his journey across the sky," she said. "We would see his reflection dancing in the waters of the Euphrates. It was a happy, peaceful time in the beginning." She sighed. "But it's all gone now. Nothing of it remains."

Old Woman sniffed, trying to hold back tears. A teardrop trickled slowly down her cheek.

"I would go so far as to say that Shuruppak was one of the most beautiful cities for its time," Utnapishtim said, casting a worried look at his wife. He knew the memories triggered her tears.

"It was the envy of the surrounding areas and so welcoming that people came from all over the place to live in it. At first, we welcomed the newcomers. But soon the city became too overcrowded with the throngs of people. Their numbers caused problems. There were too many of them. They made too much noise. The noise became unbearable.

"I did everything I could to impose order and calm throughout the city. I even tried to warn the people. I told them we were in danger of angering the gods with our noise. But nothing worked. No one paid attention to me. All my efforts to quiet the people failed miserably.

"The constant prattle of the people eventually became too loud. Just as I had feared, it disturbed the gods. The racket enraged the god Enlil who called for a council of the gods. He complained of the clamor. He grumbled mankind had become so loud and noisy that the gods were unable to get any peace and quiet. The gods agreed with him. They decided to do something about it. Together they decided to destroy all of mankind."

"What? Gilgamesh asked. "All of them? They decided to destroy all of mankind because of the clamor?"

"Yes." Utnapishtim sat up, his face tense.

"But why? Why go to such an extreme? Why kill everyone off? It seems a bit cruel, a bit unnecessary," Gilgamesh said.

"Ours is not to question the decisions of the gods," Old Woman interjected.

She was glad of the opportunity to remind Gilgamesh of an important lesson.

"We have no power to question them or to disobey them," she added, a perceptible edge in her voice.

The bitterness of her tone surprised Gilgamesh. He raised his eyebrows and scrutinized her face in search of clues that might reveal her thoughts. But her face showed no emotion. He turned to Utnapishtim.

"Go on with your story. They wanted to destroy mankind. What happened next?"

"The gods agreed to destroy mankind," Utnapishtim said. "Five of them decided to do it by causing a devastating flood. But they swore an oath to keep their plan secret to avoid the risk of interference."

"Five of the gods?" Gilgamesh asked. "Which five?"

"Anu, Enlil, Ninurta, Ennugi, and Ea," Utnapishtim replied. "But Ea was also my guardian god. He had taken an oath to protect me. Even though he took the oath of secrecy with the other gods, he had to save me. He's the cleverest of the gods is Ea. He found a way to warn me of the gods' plan without telling me directly."

"How?"

Utnapishtim didn't reply right away. He paused and looked up at his wife. Her eyes were moist. Her face expressed a profound sadness. He knew it would be painful for them to recall the flood and how it destroyed everything in its wake. No matter how many times they talked about it, the pain never seemed to get any easier. Their minds were awash with vivid memories of their friends and neighbors in a desperate struggle to survive the onslaught of the Deep. The images and sounds of people screaming for help would always haunt them. Mingled with their feelings of horror was gratitude for being spared.

"Go on," Gilgamesh said, eager to hear the rest of the story. "How did Ea warn you?"

"He came to me in a dream," Utnapishtim resumed his tale. "I dreamt I was in my reed house. Ea whispered the decision of the gods to the walls of my reed house loud enough so I could hear."

Utnapishtim took a deep breath and sighed.

"What did he say?" Gilgamesh asked, growing impatient. "What's this got to do with why the gods granted you immortality? I wish you would get to the point."

"I'm getting to it, son. Be patient. You have to hear the whole story if you want to know how the gods granted us everlasting life."

Utnapishtim paused, taking another deep breath.

"As I was saying . . ." He cast a stern look at Gilgamesh. "These were Ea's words, 'House of reeds, house of reeds, listen to what I have to say. Walls, hear me, reflect, and heed my warning. Oh, son of Ubara-Tutu! Man of Shuruppak! Tear down your house and build a boat. If you value your life, do as I say. Tear down your house and build a boat. Abandon your possessions and worldly goods. Save yourself. Build the boat so that her beam equals her length and her roof is vaulted. Then store the seed of all living creatures into the boat.'"

Utnapishtim recalled with ease the words of Ea. They were etched indelibly in his mind to be conjured up at a moment's notice. But the words always caused him to pause and reflect. Gilgamesh opened his mouth to prompt Utnapishtim to resume his story. But he caught the woman's eye. She put her finger to her lips. He snapped his mouth shut and waited until Utnapishtim was ready.

"It took me several minutes before I fully grasped Ea's command," Utnapishtim began. "I didn't question or argue with him. He's my guardian god. He was trying to save me. But I did ask his help in explaining my actions to the people and elders of Shuruppak. Ea suggested I tell them I had heard the god Enlil was angry with me. He said to tell them I had no choice but to leave the city in a hurry. I was to tell the people I had decided to travel to the Deep to live with my guardian god, Ea."

Utnapishtim sighed. He felt uneasy each time he remembered this part of the story. He had lied to people he cared about.

"Ea told me to deceive the people, to lie to them. He said I should tell them Ea had reassured me he would supply the people of Shuruppak with an abundance of fish and fowl and wheat as soon as I left them. The people believed me. They agreed to help build the boat."

"You had to deceive your own people?"

Utnapishtim nodded. He fidgeted uncomfortably in his chair.

"When the gods tell you to do something, you have to do it," Old Woman interjected.

Her voice sounded distant and hollow.

"No matter what you might think of their decision, no matter how cruel or heartless their decision might appear, you still have to obey it. You don't have a choice."

GILGAMESH OF URUK

Utnapishtim glanced at his wife, fearful she might say something unflattering about the gods. He picked up his story hurriedly to prevent her from taking off on one of her rants.

"It took us seven days to build the boat," he spoke, eager to move on to the description of the boat. "Carpenters, reed-workers, rope-makers, and even children worked on the boat. Everyone came out to help with hammering the nails, cutting the wood, carrying the tar, and making the ropes.

"We built a good, sturdy boat. It had seven decks in all, six of which were below the water level. The decks were divided into nine sections with bulkheads between each section. They measured one acre in length and across. Their sides were two hundred feet high. We plugged all the holes carefully to make the boat fully resistant to the water. We poured three thousand gallons of tar into the furnace. We used one thousand gallons of oil for caulking and stored two thousand for later use."

"Yes, yes, that's all very interesting. But what's this got to do with your being granted immortality?" Gilgamesh asked again.

"I kept all the workers well-fed and happy by slaughtering sheep and bulls for them each day. I provided them with barrels of beer, ale, and wine," Utnapishtim said. "They gobbled up the food and drank the liquids like fish in water. The atmosphere was very festive. No one suspected anything was wrong. By the seventh day, the boat was complete. We celebrated its completion as if it were the festival of the New Year."

Old Woman sighed again. Utnapishtim glanced at her. It was difficult for the two of them to recall how they had deceived their own people. But they had had no choice. Ea had decreed. They had to obey.

"I will carry the guilt with me forever," she muttered, shaking her head.

"Guilt? Why guilt?"

"Because we survived. So many people didn't."

"Yes, but it wasn't your decision," Gilgamesh reminded her. "It was the decision of the gods."

She lifted her head and looked into the distance, a vacant expression on her face.

"Launching the boat was quite a challenge," Utnapishtim continued, anxious to avoid lingering on the subject of guilt. "We rolled her forward slowly on logs until we got her into the river. I then loaded all my possessions of gold, silver, and other smaller items precious to my family. I boarded my family and kin. I boarded craftsmen and artisans. And as Ea had commanded, I boarded wild and tame animals, a male and female of every kind.

"We had barely finished loading everything on to the boat when Shamash announced it was time. He commanded me to enter the boat and seal the hatch. I asked one of the carpenters to help me seal it from outside. I rewarded him with my palace and whatever possessions I had left. I did it even though I knew only those on the boat would survive the deluge once the waters had been unleashed."

Old Woman could not contain herself. She stifled a sob while Utnapishtim stopped speaking and buried his face in his hands. Gilgamesh's patience was wearing thin. He was anxious to hear the rest of the story. But he realized these were painful memories. He waited in silence.

"And then it began," Utnapishtim said, looking up after several minutes. "It was terrifying. With the coming of dawn, the skies raged black in anger. The storm god Adad roared his deafening thunder. Shullat and Hanish, the gods of destruction, ripped through mountains and valleys demolishing everything in their wake. Then came the most terrifying part of all. The gods of the Deep arose."

Utnapishtim shivered; his hands trembled; his voice quaked.

"Nergal wrenched free the dams restraining the Waters of the Deep causing them to gush out in torrents. Ninurta opened the floodgates of the heavens and let loose the rain. The Annunaki, the seven judges of the Deep, set the land ablaze with their flaming torches.

"Adad turned daylight to darkness as he thundered onward. He smashed the land as if it were nothing bigger than a small clay cup. The storm gathered strength as the day wore on. Fierce winds blowing. Rain pouring in gushes. Floods devouring land. It was so dark with rains so heavy you couldn't even see your hand in front of you. The Deep consumed everything in its wake. No living thing was spared the onslaught. It was terrible, just terrible."

Utnapishtim breathed heavily. He shook his head and stopped speaking. Gilgamesh closed his eyes, attempting to visualize the scene.

Urshanabi had heard the story so many times before it had ceased to move him. He focused his attention on examining an ant that had crawled on to his sandals and was slowly making its way up his foot. He crushed the ant between two of his fingers and looked up to see if anyone had noticed. No one had.

All were silent, a heavy silence finally broken by the sounds of the woman weeping quietly.

"It was just horrifying," she said as she struggled to breathe between sobs. "When the waters first came, we could see the people scrambling for higher ground to escape the onslaught. But that didn't help. The waters kept coming. They kept coming and coming. As the waters got higher and higher, the people began clutching at anything they could grasp to keep them from drowning," she sobbed.

"They grabbed at each other in a frenzy," she continued. "But instead of helping one another, they just pulled each other down. Neighbors who had once helped neighbors, friends who had helped friends were now drowning each other in an attempt to save themselves. People were desperate. When it comes to self-preservation," she said, turning to face Gilgamesh, "people are capable of anything." She paused to take a deep breath.

"I couldn't bear to watch the carnage. These were some of my friends. I had known them all my life. I couldn't just stand by helplessly and let them drown. I couldn't watch them die. Mothers were holding up their babies, screaming for help. I wanted to help them. I had to do something. I ran to the hatch. I wanted to open it. I wanted to unlock the latch to let them in to shelter on the boat with us."

She began to stumble over her words. "I ran . . . I ran for the latch and I tried . . . I tried to force it open," she sobbed.

"But the waters would have come pouring in and drowned all of you on the boat," Gilgamesh said.

"I didn't care," she replied. "I didn't think about that. People were drowning. I had to try to help them. I struggled with the latch. I tried to force it open."

"Yes? What happened? You couldn't possibly have opened it. You would have drowned with the rest of them."

Old Woman buried her face in her hands. "He wouldn't let me," she said. She inclined her head toward Utnapishtim. "He grabbed me tight around the waist. I struggled and struggled. But he wouldn't let me go. He held on to me until it was too late . . . until there was no one alive left to save."

"We would have all drowned had she opened the hatch," Utnapishtim said, speaking barely above a whisper. "There was no way we could have saved everyone. And besides, we would have angered Ea. He gave me strict instructions who to let on the boat. I couldn't let her do it. I just couldn't." He shook his head.

"He grabbed me and wouldn't let me go," she repeated. Her voice quivered. Her eyes stared into space as if focusing intensely on something in the distance. But there was nothing there. Only empty space.

"I struggled to get free, to get to the latch and open it. But I couldn't," she stuttered in between the sobs. "He held on to me tightly. All I could do was watch the horror and hear the screams. The screams. I can still hear the screams.

"The women, the children, our friends, our neighbors, people we had known all our lives. All gone. Swallowed up by the waters before our eyes. And when it became too dark to see, all we could hear were their screams for help. They were drowning," she repeated. "There was nothing we could do about it. Nothing," she sobbed. "Everything was lost. And then it became quiet. The silence was deafening. It told us everything . . . everything we didn't want to know," Old Woman said, tears streaming down her face.

She turned to Gilgamesh.

"Believe me when I tell you this, son. There are things worse than death. I'll carry the image of our friends drowning in the Waters of the Deep forever. It will haunt me forever. I'll never be rid of it. To this day I sometimes wake up at night hearing their screams for help. Son, believe me when I tell you. There are things far worse than death."

Chapter 19: The Aftermath

She took a deep breath to arrest the flow of tears. The silence weighed heavily in the room. Urshanabi stopped fidgeting and sat perfectly still. Gilgamesh lowered his eyes as if trying to visualize the event. Finally, Utnapishtim spoke up, wringing his hands as he spoke.

"The devastation was everywhere," he said. "The flood waters got to be so high even the gods were terrified by the havoc they had unleashed. Ea told me the gods were afraid. They fled to Anu's palace in the heavens to escape from the raging waters. But Anu had also witnessed the rising of the waters. He was afraid. He thought the waters would reach his palace. He had locked the gates to keep the waters out. He refused to open the doors even when the rest of the gods showed up on his doorstep and banged on his door. The gods pleaded with him to let them in. But he wouldn't do it. The gods had nowhere to hide. They cowered in front of the gates of Anu's palace like petrified animals."

Urshanabi couldn't suppress a small chuckle. He had heard the story so many times before. But each time Utnapishtim got to the part of the gods cringing with fear at the havoc they had created, he always laughed. He had confided to Old Woman in the past he thought it served the gods right. But he never dared to say so in front of Utnapishtim.

Old Woman glanced at Gilgamesh and observed the corners of his mouth turned up into a weak smile. She couldn't resist a small smile herself as she thought of the gods cringing with fear. Fortunately, she had the sense to keep her thoughts to herself.

"The gods were terrified," Utnapishtim said. "They regretted the devastation."

Old Woman shrugged her shoulders. She couldn't help but scoff at the thought of the gods showing compassion to humans. She challenged Utnapishtim.

"If they felt such remorse, why did they do it in the first place? Why did they have to kill off so many people? Why innocent children? Why babies? What harm had babies ever done to the gods?"

Utnapishtim pretended not to hear. None of his answers had satisfied her in the past. He knew they weren't going to satisfy her now. He ignored the interruption.

"Ea told me Aruru, the mother of men, was the first to express regret. She screamed like a woman giving birth. 'If only I had never spoken up in the council of the gods,' she cried. 'If only I had never agreed to destroy all of mankind. How could I have done this?' she wailed. 'How could I have agreed to destroy my children for are these not my children? I gave birth to the human race. And yet I agreed to send down the great flood to destroy them. Now they are floating in the waters like dead fish. What have we done?' she cried out to the gods. The other gods lamented with her. They regretted their actions. They wept bitter tears."

Utnapishtim sighed and took a deep breath. His voice was hoarse.

"It was too late to change anything," he said. "The damage was done. All we could do was wait it out."

Gilgamesh was about to open his mouth. He caught the old woman's eye and decided against it. He waited in silence.

"The storm continued for six days and seven nights," Utnapishtim said. "After the storm had abated and the rains stopped, the ocean grew calm. But nothing had survived outside the boat. All we could see in every direction was water. There was not a trace of land anywhere in sight.

"When I thought it was safe, I climbed up and struggled to open the hatch. It was tightly sealed. I was able to loosen the latch eventually. I pried it open. I didn't know what to expect. I pushed open the hatch. I saw a clear blue sky. I felt the warmth of the sun on my face. The worst was over. I collapsed on my knees. I called out to Wife. She came running. She looked out at the open hatch. She saw the sun and sky. She put her arms around me. We wept."

Gilgamesh leaned back in his chair and sighed.

"That was quite an experience," he said, a slight quiver in his voice. "I don't know how anyone could have survived it. The gods must love you dearly to let you survive such an ordeal."

"Ha!" Old Woman couldn't stop herself. "Yes, indeed, the gods must love us dearly." She sneered, unable to conceal the bitterness in her voice. "Don't you understand what happened? The gods lost all control of the flood once they set things in motion. It was so bad they even scared themselves. They tried to escape to Anu's palace in the heavens to get away from the fury they'd unleashed. The whole place was devastated. Nothing left. Dead bodies floated in the water everywhere you looked."

"Yes, but they allowed you to survive," Gilgamesh insisted.

"We survived, but our survival had little to do with the gods. We were on our own as soon as the skies opened and the flood began. The gods didn't protect us. They were too busy protecting themselves. They abandoned us. We survived in spite of them."

Her voice dripped with sarcasm.

"Yes, indeed," she said. "The gods must love us dearly."

"Now, Wife," Utnapishtim admonished her. "You know as well as I do the gods love us. You know it's wrong to accuse them of abandoning us. If it hadn't been for Ea's warning, we would have drowned with the rest of Shuruppak."

"I know. I know. But did they have to destroy everything? Did they have to create a storm so fierce it terrified even them? I can still see it as if it were happening right in front of me."

She covered her eyes trying to block out the images.

"The children desperately latching on to the nearest adult they could find; the mothers holding up their babies, pleading for us to save them. It was horrible! Just horrible! I'll never get those images out of my mind. Never."

"I thought you said earlier we shouldn't question the gods," Gilgamesh said, turning to look at her. His eyes stared at her expectantly. "So why are you questioning them now?"

A smirk scrawled across his face. He looked pleased with himself. That will show her, he thought. That will get back at her for all the times she made me squirm, for all the times she probed me with questions I couldn't answer.

"You're right." Old Woman said. Her brow wrinkled into a deep frown. She raised her head. Tears streamed down her face unchecked. She didn't bother to wipe them away.

"I did say that. And I believe we shouldn't question them. But this is so difficult to understand. They wreaked havoc on us. They destroyed everything and everyone. No one survived except for those of us on the boat."

"Yes, but the gods rewarded us with eternal life," Utnapishtim reminded her. He inclined his head toward her. "We're thankful to them for giving us immortality." He spoke as if he were addressing a young child.

"Of all those who survived the flood, we were the only two selected by the gods to receive eternal life. We must be thankful to the gods. They gave us a gift they withheld from all other living creatures."

Old Woman didn't respond right away. She lowered her eyes, wiped the tears with the sleeve of her robe, and cradled her face in her hands. She lifted her head to look into Utnapishtim's eyes. She knew he wanted her to echo his words of gratitude.

"Is it such a gift, after all?" she asked.

Utnapishtim pleaded with his eyes for her to say no more. He was afraid for the two of them if she declared her misgivings. But she ignored his plea just as she had done many times before. She spoke her mind.

"Was it worth it?" she asked. "Was it worth it after the horrors we witnessed? We will live forever, but so will our memories. They'll never fade. We witnessed a terrifying ordeal, an ordeal that killed almost everyone we ever knew. It completely shattered our former lives. Was it worth it?"

She paused, breathing heavily. "I don't know." She shook her head repeatedly. "I've asked myself that same question every day since it happened. I still don't know the answer. I probably never will. I just wonder sometimes if it had been better for us to have died, to have perished with our friends and neighbors. At least we wouldn't be haunted by these terrible memories."

"You mustn't say that," Utnapishtim reproached her, speaking in a loud whisper. "You mustn't appear ungrateful. We were singled out by the gods. We were granted immortality," he repeated. "We must be thankful."

She managed a weak smile. She nodded her head.

"If you say so," she replied. "You're probably right."

"You know I'm right," Utnapishtim said.

"How did the gods grant you eternal life?" Gilgamesh asked, wanting to get back to the issue that concerned him the most. "Did they come down from the heavens and talk to you?"

"It didn't happen quite that way, son," Utnapishtim sighed.

"Well, go on with your story," Gilgamesh said, his impatience palpable.

"Yes, yes, of course," Utnapishtim replied. "Now, where was I?"

"You opened the hatch and saw the sunlight. What happened after that?" Gilgamesh asked.

"The first thing I had to do was determine if land was visible anywhere. I looked around and saw a coast in the distance. The boat drifted toward it. Then it ran aground on top of Mount Nisir. The mountain clung to the boat and wouldn't release it. We remained stuck there for six days and seven nights, unable to move."

"And that's when the gods came down and granted you immortality?" Gilgamesh interrupted him.

"Not exactly, son. Be patient. I'm getting there," Utnapishtim replied. "As I was saying. On the morning of the seventh day, I released a dove. She flew off looking for land. Finding none, she returned to the boat. The next time I released a swallow. The same thing happened. The swallow flew off looking for land. Finding none, she returned to the boat. I waited for a while and then tried again. This time I released a raven. By now the waters had begun to recede. The raven flew off and found a tree branch. I could see her in the distance. She sat on the branch, ate some food, and then flew away. She didn't come back. I took it as a sign the waters had receded sufficiently for the raven to find land. I knew it was now safe for us to leave the boat. I opened the doors and freed the animals.

"The first thing I did was to thank the gods," he said, glancing at his wife. "Yes, we had to thank the gods," he repeated. "It was important to thank the gods. After all, they had saved us from drowning." He looked at her to see if she would offer any resistance to his words. But she had nothing more to say. She bowed her head in silence.

"So that's when the gods came down," Gilgamesh sighed.

"I offered a sacrifice to the gods in gratitude," Utnapishtim continued, ignoring the interruption. "I slaughtered a sheep on the mountain top for the gods. I followed the ritual by setting up two rows of seven cauldrons. I burned reeds, cedar, and branches of myrtle. When the gods smelled the sweet aroma of burning leaves and roasting meat, they knew it was safe to come down from the heavens. They descended upon me like a hoard of flies. They were starving because they'd been deprived of food since the onset of the flood. They gathered around the sacrifice and offerings I had prepared for them. They devoured the food. They were hungry. They were grateful."

"Ah," said Gilgamesh, leaning back in his chair. "So that's why they decided to grant you immortality."

"Be patient, son. We're not quite there yet," Utnapishtim replied.

Chapter 20: The Pact

Utnapishtim looked around. Old Woman was gently rocking her body in slow, rhythmic motions. Her eyes were lowered, her head bowed. Relieved that she had stopped weeping, Utnapishtim turned his gaze to where Urshanabi sat in his chair. Look at that fool! he thought. He's so relaxed, gazing innocently into space. He looks as if he doesn't have a care in the world. He probably thinks I've forgotten the terrible thing he did by bringing Gilgamesh here. Well, he's wrong. That's not something I will easily forget or forgive. But I'll deal with him later, he decided.

Utnapishtim turned to face Gilgamesh. The young man sat on the edge of his seat, anxious to hear the rest of the story. He's waiting for me to tell him how I overcame death, thought Utnapishtim. I feel sorry for the poor boy. He thinks he'll be able to do the same thing I did. He thinks he can cheat death. Well, he's in for a disappointment. Not much I can do about it. I better get this over with. Maybe then the boy will leave us alone. Maybe then he'll go home.

Utnapishtim shrugged his shoulders. He took a deep breath and picked up his story.

"The gods smelled the sweet aroma of the burning incense and the succulent meat roasting on the fire. They came down from the heavens one at a time. The first to appear was the goddess Aruru. She took off her beautiful necklace of lapis lazuli, the one Anu had given her when they were courting. She held it up to the sky so all could witness the pact she made with humans."

"Is this it? Is this where she granted you immortality?" Gilgamesh interrupted him, unable to contain his excitement.

"Not yet, son," Utnapishtim replied. "I'm getting there. Just show a little patience."

"All right," Gilgamesh said, bowing his head. "I'm sorry. I won't interrupt you again."

"Good," Utnapishtim said. "Now, where was I? Oh, yes, Aruru held up her necklace and declared her pact for all the gods to hear."

Utnapishtim glanced at Gilgamesh to make sure he wasn't about to interrupt him again. Gilgamesh bobbed his head up and down eagerly, but he remained quiet.

"So Aruru held up her necklace and declared her pact," Utnapishtim repeated. "I'm not sure I remember her exact words, but she said something along the lines of, 'By this necklace that Anu gave me as a token of his love, I swear I'll never forget what has happened here. I swear never again will I allow another flood to destroy my children.'"

"And you were there the whole time?" Gilgamesh asked. "You heard her making this pact?"

"Yes." Utnapishtim nodded.

"Well, that's a relief. At least we know we'll never have to endure another devastating flood," Gilgamesh said.

"Yes, but who knows what method the gods will come up with the next time they decide to punish humans," Old Woman interjected. "They might decide to do something even worse." She made no attempt to conceal the bitterness she felt.

"Then Aruru invited the other gods to join her at the sacrifice," Utnapishtim continued. He didn't even look at his wife. "She invited all the gods with the exception of Enlil. She said he was not welcome there since he had caused the flood. 'He was reckless,' she said. She sounded angry and bitter. 'He tried to destroy all my children. What he did was unforgiveable.' The other gods agreed and came down for the meal."

Utnapishtim paused. He took a deep breath.

"And then Enlil showed up," he said. "He looked around. He saw the ship. He saw that some of us had survived the flood. He saw Wife and I standing on the boat. He erupted in a rage. 'What's this ship doing here?' he seethed. 'Why are these humans still alive? How did they survive?' He demanded answers from the gods. 'The great flood was to destroy every single one of them,' he insisted. 'Who helped these humans survive?'

"Old Woman and I just stood there, our heads bowed, our eyes lowered. We trembled, afraid to look at Enlil, afraid to speak, afraid to move, terrified he would destroy us in his rage. He spoke with such anger. I suspect the other gods were afraid to reply to him. Ninurta was the first to summon the courage to reply.

"'Who is the cleverest god that can outsmart us all?' he asked. 'It was none other than Ea. Ea it was who devised a scheme to save these humans.'

"Enlil was furious. But Ea confronted him before he said anything. 'You're the bravest and strongest of the gods,' Ea flattered him. 'How could you do this? How could you send a deluge to destroy all of mankind?'

"'But they were making too much noise,' Enlil protested. 'You heard their racket. It was intolerable. They wouldn't give us any peace. We had to do something to shut them up. We had to restore peace and quiet.'

"'You're justified in punishing a criminal for his crime and a wicked person for his wickedness,' Ea said. 'But you had no right to punish all of mankind for the wickedness of a few. Was it right to try to kill all of them when only some had offended us?' he asked. 'Is it fair to lash out with punishment for all in this way? No, Enlil. You should have shown mercy. You should have been lenient.'

"'You say that now," Enlil said. 'But you didn't object before when I suggested the destruction of mankind. None of you objected when I suggested sending a flood,' he said to the gods. 'Why didn't you say something then? If you didn't want me to send a flood, what should I have done?' he asked, his voice still seething with anger.

"'Any number of things,' Ea replied. 'You could have sent lions or wolves or a famine or even a deadly plague. That would have killed some of them. But it would have left a great many others to survive. You could have even sent a flood but not such a devastating one to cause them all to die. But you had to go to the extreme. You tried to destroy them all, Enlil. That was wrong of you. Very, very wrong.'"

"That must have enraged Enlil even more," Gilgamesh said. "I'm guessing he didn't like the criticism."

"No, he didn't," Utnapishtim replied. "Enlil was not easily subdued. He confronted Ea. 'You took an oath with four other gods to keep the flood a secret,' he said. 'You broke your word. You betrayed us,' he accused him.

"'I did not break my word,' Ea protested. 'I kept my oath. I didn't reveal the secret of the flood to Utnapishtim or to any other mortal. I just whispered it to the walls of his reed house. Utnapishtim happened to overhear me in his dream. I can't be blamed for that. It's not my fault the man has such good hearing.'"

Utnapishtim chuckled. It was Ea's quick-thinking trickery that had saved their lives.

"Enlil didn't reply right away,' Utnapishtim continued. "Wife and I just stood there. I could feel our bodies trembling with fear. We waited not knowing if Enlil would take his anger out on us. He seemed to be brooding about what had happened. That's when Ea

GILGAMESH OF URUK

spoke up, again. I guess he realized it would be to no one's advantage to have the gods feuding among themselves. He offered Enlil a chance to redeem himself, a way to reconcile their differences. He entrusted him with power to decide our fate. He put us entirely at Enlil's mercy. He said to him, 'Since it was you who caused the flood, you get to decide what's to become of these two humans. The choice is yours.'"

By this time, Gilgamesh was perched precariously on the very edge of his seat. He stood up and started pacing nervously in the room. This must be it, he thought. At last I get to hear how Utnapishtim was able to cheat death. He wanted to ask many questions but decided to wait in silence to avoid offending the old man.

"Old Woman and I were scared," Utnapishtim continued. "I gripped her hand expecting the worst. We thought Enlil would vent his anger at us. We thought he would strike us down right then and there. But Enlil surprised us. He heard Ea's invitation to decide our fate. He became pensive. We waited, afraid to breathe, afraid to move.

"Enlil boarded the boat and walked toward us. I tightened my grip on Old Woman's hand. I was certain we were to die. Enlil came forward and faced us. I held my breath. We trembled. Enlil took my hand. He led me off the boat to stand near the gods. Then he boarded the boat again. He took Old Woman by the hand. He led her off the boat. He made her stand by my side. He commanded us both to kneel down in front of him."

Gilgamesh was beside himself with anticipation. He stopped pacing and stood at attention, anxious to hear Utnapishtim's words. Utnapishtim sensed his excitement. He felt sorry for the young man. He knew he would soon be facing disappointment. There's no point delaying the inevitable any longer, he thought.

175

"We did as we were commanded to do. We knelt down in front of Enlil," Utnapishtim said. "He came and wedged himself between us. Then, touching each of our foreheads, he gave us his blessing. He pronounced these words to the gods, 'Hear me, oh gods,' he said. 'Up until now, Utnapishtim and his wife have been mortals. They were destined to live and die at the time and place appointed by the gods. This is the lot of all mortals. But today I declare Utnapishtim and his wife will shed their mortal skin. They will become as gods. They will be like us. They will never die. They will live forever.'"

Utnapishtim took a deep breath. He looked directly at Gilgamesh.

"There you have it, son," he said. "You came all this way to hear our story, and now you've heard it all. You've heard all about the flood. You've heard how it killed the people of Shuruppak except for those of us on the boat. Ea, my guardian god, warned me and saved our lives. After it was all over, the gods came down from the heavens. They gathered around the sacrifice. Enlil joined them. He was angry that we had survived. But then he granted Wife and I immortality. All the gods nodded their approval. They brought Old Woman and I to Dilmun, to this faraway place at the source of the river to live. We are to live here for all eternity. This is where we've lived ever since. So here we are, son. There is nothing more to tell. You've heard our story. You have answers to the questions you came all this way to seek."

Utnapishtim sat back in his chair. His wife sighed and looked up at him. Gilgamesh was about to speak when Utnapishtim intercepted him.

"Son, now you know how Old Woman and I survived the flood. You know how we cheated death. Let me ask you a question. What good has this knowledge done you?"

"What do you mean?"

"What I mean," Utnapishtim said, "is simply this. Has it brought you any closer to cheating death? If so, how do you plan to do it? How are you going to assemble the gods on your behalf? How are you going to get them to agree to grant you immortality? And if you can't assemble them yourself, who is going to assemble them for you? Who is going to convince them you're worthy of becoming a god?"

Gilgamesh walked with faltering steps back to his chair and sat down. His mind was in a fog. He shook his head. He looked puzzled, bewildered.

"Well," he faltered. "I don't know. I need time to think about this," he said. "There must be some way. I just need time to think."

"You do that, son," Utnapishtim mocked him. "Take all the time you need. And when you come up with a solution, let me know."

A look of concern swept across Old Woman's face when she saw a deflated Gilgamesh struggling to come to terms with Utnapishtim's taunts.

"Now, now, Utnapishtim," she interjected. She felt sorry for the boy and was anxious to intercede on his behalf. "There's no need to be so smug about it."

"There's no need to be like what?" Utnapishtim snapped. "I don't know what you mean. I was just being honest and straightforward with the boy. He needs to hear the truth. I warned him when I first saw him down at the beach. I told him he would never be able to cheat death. But would he listen? Would he believe me? Oh, no. Not him. He was too smart for that. He thought he could do anything. He didn't believe a word I said. Well, now he's heard it all. He's heard how we survived the flood, how we cheated death. Let's see what brilliant plan he comes up with to cheat his own death. Let's sit back and wait, shall we? You and I are in no hurry. We have all the time in the world."

"He came all this way to hear our story," Old Woman replied in a calm voice to soften the harshness of Utnapishtim's words. "We owed it to him to tell him what happened to us. And now he has heard our story. Give him time to accept it. Give him time to think about what he should do."

"Well," Utnapishtim said. "I can tell him what he should do. He should turn around and go back where he came from. And I can tell you one thing he shouldn't have done. He should never have come here in the first place. And if it weren't for that fool," he snarled, nodding at Urshanabi, "he would never have been able to cross the Waters of Death alive."

Urshanabi sank further down in his chair and fidgeted uncomfortably. He was afraid to speak in his own defense. He wished he could crawl back into the wall and hide rather than have to contend with Utnapishtim's anger again. Meanwhile, Gilgamesh sat in a daze, unable to speak. It was up to the old woman to ease the tension.

"Husband!" she said, raising her voice. "We have been through Urshanabi's role in this already. There's no need to bring it back up again."

"Yes, yes. Whatever you say," Utnapishtim replied, his tone brusque. "So, here we are. Gilgamesh came all this way to hear our story. Now he's heard it. I hope he finally understands the gods' gift of immortality was a one-time happening. I hope he realizes he will never be able to get them to repeat it. So, what happens now? What's he going to do now he knows his fate is to die like all other mortals?" He paused and faced Gilgamesh. "What are you going to do, Gilgamesh?" he taunted him.

Old Woman didn't approve of Utnapishtim's tone, but she knew he was right. Gilgamesh had to face the truth. He had finally heard their story. He had to decide on his next move. She looked at him, hoping he would say something.

Gilgamesh had buried his face in his hands, listening to the exchange between the old man and his wife. He was at a loss. He had come all this way and now he had to go back where he came from. The only thing he could take back with him was the story of how Utnapishtim and the woman had survived the flood. Nothing more. His whole journey seemed futile.

He stood up abruptly and paced the room. His steps were hurried. His mind raced in different directions. He wrung his hands. He went through the sequence of events searching for answers. The flood. The boat. Devastation. The gods' remorse. Utnapishtim and Old Woman. Aruru's pact. Enlil's anger. Immortality. His mind twisted summersaults as he paced the room faster than before, his thoughts in turmoil, grappling their way around the dilemma. The gods will not make me the same offer they made to Utnapishtim, he thought. I'm going to die. Just like Enkidu. Just like all other mortals. There must be some other way around this. What am I going to do? I refuse to die. I refuse to accept this.

"What are we to do with him?" Utnapishtim asked his wife when Gilgamesh failed to answer.

She shook her head. She peered at Gilgamesh, a weary look in her eyes. She shifted her gaze away from him. She didn't know what more could be done. She turned to look at him again. He was still pacing the floor, wringing his hands.

"We must send him home," she said. "Gilgamesh must go home."

Chapter 21: The Sleep

"I don't know," Gilgamesh mumbled under his breath. He shook his head in despair. "I don't know what to do."

Old Woman glanced at Utnapishtim. "Is there nothing we can do to help him before sending him off? There must be something," she said.

"What do you expect me to do?" Utnapishtim's tone was gruff. "I can't summon the gods. I can't make them grant him eternal life. There's nothing I can do." He shrugged his shoulders in frustration.

A heavy silence descended upon the room. No one knew what to say. Urshanabi sat still, afraid to move or to draw attention to himself. Gilgamesh stopped pacing and stood in the corner of the room, his face buried in his hands. He couldn't bring himself to look up.

Utnapishtim and the old woman exchanged glances. She nodded in the direction of the young man. She mouthed the words, "Do something," to Utnapishtim. He shook his head. She waited. Finally, he spoke up.

"There is one thing we can try," he said, turning to face Gilgamesh. Gilgamesh put his hands down and looked at Utnapishtim.

"Yes?"

"You might be able to get around this. There just might be a way."

"Yes?" Gilgamesh said, his tone hopeful.

"You have to pass a test to prove yourself worthy. You have to prove to the gods you deserve the gift of immortality," Utnapishtim replied.

"Yes, yes, I'll do it," Gilgamesh said. "I'll take the test."

"Son, you don't know what the test is yet," Utnapishtim reminded him.

"It doesn't matter what it is. I'll do it. I know I can do it. I'm the strongest man alive. I can do anything," Gilgamesh replied.

"Wait a minute, son," Old Woman said, shaking her head. She wanted to stop the foolish boy before he committed to some impossible task. "Be patient. Let's see what this test is before you go bragging about your ability to pass it. You would think after all you've been through you could show a little more humility."

"It doesn't matter," Gilgamesh retorted. "I can pass this test," he said, without a hint of hesitation in his voice. "I can do it. I can pass any test you give me. What's this test, Utnapishtim?"

"Prove to the gods you deserve immortality," Utnapishtim said. "Prove to them you are unlike any other mortal. Stay awake for the next seven days. Deprive yourself of sleep for seven continuous days. If you can resist giving in to sleep, you might be able to resist giving in to death. Maybe, just maybe, if you pass the test, the gods may deem you worthy of immortality."

"I can do it," Gilgamesh said excitedly. "I can resist sleep. I am not in the least bit tired. If I can run for twelve continuous hours through the tunnel of the Deep, I can do this easily enough. I used to go for days without sleep in Uruk," he bragged. "It will be easy for me."

Old Woman looked at Utnapishtim. She knew the test was ridiculous. There was no possible way the foolish boy could stay awake for that long. She ignored his childish display of bravado.

"Utnapishtim, be reasonable," she said. "That's an impossible task. Every mortal has the need for sleep. Can't you give him a test he has at least some chance of passing?"

"No. The test has to be challenging or it won't prove anything. He has to prove himself capable. He wants to rise above his mortality. Let him demonstrate to the gods he is worthy of their gift. You can't make the test too easy. And, besides, you heard him say he won't have any difficulty passing the test."

"Husband," she said sternly. "Look at him. He's already exhausted from his travels. How can you expect him to pass this test? You know as well as I do no mortal can overcome the need to sleep, let alone someone who has traveled as many days as Gilgamesh."

"Well, if you believe what he's telling us, you know Gilgamesh says he can easily overcome sleep." Utnapishtim smirked. He was obviously relishing this. "I believe him. And you should, too. We've no reason to doubt him. You heard him boast earlier he never needed sleep in Uruk. He was immune to it. Remember that? Remember how he bragged he could stay awake all night and never tire? I am sure this test will be easy enough for him."

"I remember him saying that," Urshanabi said, jumping in to participate. "I remember him boasting he never needed sleep. He told us he spent his nights enjoying the first right with each virgin bride and he would follow it with feasting and celebration all night long. I'm sure this will be an easy test for Gilgamesh."

Old Woman scowled at Urshanabi. She recognized a trap when she saw it. She was about to protest when Gilgamesh intercepted her.

"That's right," he said. "I never needed sleep then. And I don't need it now. I'm strong. I can easily prevail against sleep. Just watch me do it."

Old Woman looked at him with a weariness in her eyes. The foolish boy spoke such nonsense, she thought. She shook her head.

"Son," she said, "your pride is getting in the way of your thinking again. Haven't you learned anything from your mistakes? Hasn't your pride gotten you in enough trouble already? Be sensible. You're exhausted. You can't go without sleep for one day, let alone for seven days. Ask for another test."

"You're wrong," Gilgamesh insisted. "I can do this easily enough. I have gone for days at a time without sleep. I've done it before. I can do it again. Just watch me."

She tried one more time with Utnapishtim.

"Give him another test," she pleaded. "Give him one that he has a chance of passing."

"Why should I? You heard what he said. He can pass this test easily enough. He's done it before. He can do it again. Gilgamesh is so strong. He is so tough—tougher than any man alive. He won't find it difficult at all to be deprived of sleep. Isn't that right, Gilgamesh?"

"That's right. I know I have the strength to do this," Gilgamesh insisted.

Old Woman's brow tensed into an angry scowl. It was useless to convince Gilgamesh. His arrogance had reared its ugly head again. She argued with Utnapishtim. They bickered back and forth for several minutes. She told him the test was unfair. He insisted it was perfectly fair. She was determined to save the boy from failure. She felt he had suffered enough already. He was determined to knock the boy down, to teach him a lesson.

There was a lull in the conversation. They had reached an impasse. It was then they heard heavy breathing. They exchanged glances and turned slowly to look at Gilgamesh. He was slouched in his chair, snoring softly.

Utnapishtim looked back at his wife. Nodding his head, he couldn't resist a triumphant smirk.

"It's just as I expected," he said.

Old Woman glared at him. She said nothing.

"I can't believe it. He's fallen asleep," Urshanabi whispered. "I don't understand. Why did he fall asleep?

He bragged he could stay awake for days at time. What happened? Wasn't he speaking the truth when he told us these things?"

"Yes, he was speaking the truth, all right, at least what was true for him at the time," Utnapishtim replied. "He most probably could stay awake for days at a time when he was in Uruk. But something changed in Gilgamesh after he met Enkidu."

"What changed?" Urshanabi said. "When did it change? I don't understand. What happened? What do you mean?"

"He lost some of his strength. He lost some of those qualities that made him more god than man," Utnapishtim replied.

"What? How? When? He didn't say anything about losing any of his strength."

"He's probably not aware of it, himself. But if you listened to his story carefully, you would have figured it out. He lost some of his strength just as Enkidu did."

"Huh? When? How?" Urshanabi was baffled. "When did Enkidu lose his animal strength? I don't remember hearing that. I don't remember Gilgamesh saying anything about that."

"Yes, you do," Utnapishtim said. "Think about it. Do you remember Gilgamesh saying Enkidu was strong in the wilderness? He could outrun the animals?"

"Yes."

"And what happened to Enkidu after he and Shamhat had lain together?"

"He couldn't keep up with the animals anymore," Urshanabi replied. "They were too fast for him. He went back to Shamhat and sat at her feet."

Urshanabi paused for a minute to reflect.

"Oh, now I see," he said. "I get it. Enkidu lost some of his strength. Lying with Shamhat was the beginning of his initiation into manhood. But it also sapped his animal strength. Enkidu had become physically weaker than he was before."

"That's right." Utnapishtim nodded his head. "And just as Enkidu lost some of his strength through intimacy with Shamhat, Gilgamesh lost some of his strength through intimacy with Enkidu. His god-like qualities were depleted, including his ability to stay awake."

"What? I don't remember that. When did that happen? How do you know this? I don't remember him saying anything like that. Do you mean Gilgamesh is no longer part god?" Urshanabi asked, still baffled.

"Think, Urshanabi," Utnapishtim said, growing increasingly frustrated. "Use your brain. Do you remember him telling us about the journey to Humbaba?"

"Yes," Urshanabi replied, frowning, trying hard to recall the details.

"Well, what happened at the end of each day while they were on that journey?"

"They set up their shelter for the night. They offered libations to the gods. Then Gilgamesh fell asleep and had a dream. Enkidu interpreted the dream for him. And the same thing happened the next day. And the day after that. And the day . . ."

Urshanabi stopped mid-sentence. His eyes grew wide. He shouted the words in his excitement.

"He fell asleep! Gilgamesh fell asleep each night. Now I remember. He needed sleep at the end of the day. He was just like the rest of us. He had lost his god-like qualities."

"Urshanabi, lower your voice," Old Woman reprimanded him. "There's no need to shout. You'll wake him up. The poor boy is exhausted. He needs his sleep."

"Wake him up? All the shouting in the world couldn't wake him up," Utnapishtim scoffed. "Not even another flood would wake that boy up. I don't know what you're so worried about. The boy will probably sleep for days at a time. You wait and see."

"That may very well be," she said, speaking in a loud whisper. "But I don't want to risk it. The boy has been through a lot. The least we can do is lower our voices to give him a chance to get some uninterrupted sleep."

"Sorry, Mother." Urshanabi lowered his voice. "I'll be quieter."

Turning to Utnapishtim, he asked, "So that's when you knew he had become more human? When he traveled with Enkidu to the Cedar Forest?"

"That's right," Utnapishtim said. "He had lost some of his god-like qualities. He needed his sleep just like every other human. That's how I knew he would never pass the test. He was weaker. The problem is he has yet to recognize it about himself. He thinks he's still invincible."

"So you set up a test you knew he would fail. You want him to realize he's more human than god-like. Is that why you tricked him into believing he could pass the test?"

"Well, I didn't exactly trick him," Utnapishtim protested. "He tricked himself. He still believes he is capable of doing anything. But Gilgamesh has changed. He can no longer go without sleep. His intimacy with Enkidu changed him just as Enkidu's intimacy with Shamhat brought about his change. There's no going back to his original state. Gilgamesh has to realize that. It's the only way he'll come to terms with his own mortality. All this searching about for immortality, all this thinking he can cheat death. It's not going to get him anywhere. He needs to see that. He needs to accept it once and for all. He needs to get on with his life instead of whimpering like a child."

"Do you think he understands that now?" Urshanabi asked, speaking barely above a whisper.

"I don't know. We'll have to see when he wakes up. I explained it to him several times. He just didn't believe me. Maybe he'll believe me now."

"I'm so surprised," Urshanabi said. "To think Gilgamesh could have lost some of his strength because of his intimacy with Enkidu. I never figured any of this out."

"No, I know you didn't," Utnapishtim said. "But she did." He nodded toward the old woman.

She lowered her eyes. She didn't have the heart to speak. She turned her head slowly to look at Gilgamesh. He was sleeping soundly on the chair, his breathing soft and rhythmic.

Chapter 22: The Loaves of Bread

The three of them stared at Gilgamesh. He was slouched in his chair, his head tilting heavily to one side. He must be very uncomfortable, thought Old Woman. She got up slowly and gathered soft pillows and blankets. She laid them on the floor in the corner of the room.

"Urshanabi," she said. "Help me to get him to the bed. "You, too, Utnapishtim. We need you to help us carry him so he can lie down."

"Why?" Utnapishtim grumbled. "Why can't you just leave him be where he is?"

"Because this is no way to sleep. He'll wake up with a sore body and a stiff neck. For once in your life, please don't argue with me. Do as I say."

Urshanabi stood up and walked toward Gilgamesh. Utnapishtim remained seated, reluctant to help. Old Woman persisted.

"Utnapishtim, get up and help. I cannot lift him. You have to help us get him to the bed."

Reluctantly Utnapishtim got up, muttering incoherently under his breath.

"Wife, you never give me any peace."

He shuffled slowly toward Gilgamesh.

"Urshanabi, I'll lift him from under his arms, you lift him from his feet," he grumbled.

Together, they lifted Gilgamesh and hobbled slowly to the makeshift bed the woman had prepared for him. Gilgamesh was heavier than he looked. Utnapishtim found it difficult to hold on to him. He staggered across the room barely able to keep a grip on Gilgamesh's arms. They no sooner got to the bed than Utnapishtim lost his grip on Gilgamesh's body. The young man's torso slipped through his fingers. He landed on the makeshift bed with a thump. It wasn't as soft a landing

GILGAMESH OF URUK

as the woman would have liked. She watched, anxious the bumpy landing may have woken up the young man. But Gilgamesh was sound asleep. He groaned softly and turned over on his side.

"Careful," she whispered. "You'll wake him up."

"I doubt it," scoffed Utnapishtim making his way back to his seat. "It'll take Adad and all his thundering storm clouds to wake this boy up. And maybe not even then."

Old Woman got down on her knees. Her touch was gentle as she maneuvered Gilgamesh's head comfortably on the pillow. She covered him with a light blanket. She stood up and stepped back slowly, reassuring herself his sleep was full of quiet, regular breathing. She then went back to her seat.

"What now?" Utnapishtim asked. "What do we do now? We can't just let him stay here."

"For now we leave him to sleep. When he's ready, he'll wake up," she replied. "Until then, we try not to disturb him."

"He'll probably sleep for days," Utnapishtim complained.

"Well, so what? Let him sleep," she insisted. "He needs it. He's been through a lot."

"Yes, but he'll deny he ever slept," Utnapishtim replied. "You wait and see if I'm not right. You have a forgiving nature, Wife. You don't understand these people."

"And what types of people might that be?" she said, arching her eyebrows.

"Arrogant people. People who think the rules don't apply to them. People who think they're better than the rest of us," Utnapishtim replied.

"Utnapishtim, he's just a boy," she said, the corners of her mouth turning up into a smile. "I won't deny he's arrogant. I won't deny his pride has gotten him into a whole mess of trouble. But he's just a boy. He's been through a lot. He'll learn. Give him time."

"I don't want to give him time," Utnapishtim argued. "He's not my problem. He should never have come here in the first place. I'm telling you he can't be trusted. You've not dealt with people like him before. I have. They're all alike. They're arrogant. And they're liars. Gilgamesh is no different. He'll wake up and deny he ever slept."

"You may be right. But for now, let's just let him sleep."

Old Woman shook her head. She disapproved of Utnapishtim's suspicious nature. She knew his tendency was to distrust people, to see the worst in them. She ignored his remarks and busied herself with puttering about the house.

Utnapishtim's brow wrinkled into the beginning of a frown. He slouched in his chair, lost in thought. Suddenly he sat up, smiling.

"I've got it. I know what we can do," he said. "Wife, bake a loaf of bread for each day Gilgamesh is asleep. Line up the loaves next to his bed so he sees them when he wakes up. Put a mark on the wall for each loaf of bread you bake. That way he'll be able to count for himself the number of days he slept. He won't have to take our word for it. And he won't be able to deny it."

She nodded her head. "That's a good idea."

"You needn't sound so surprised. It does happen sometimes," Utnapishtim said in an injured tone. "I do get the occasional good idea, you know."

"I didn't mean it like that," she said. "Of course, you get good ideas. I didn't mean it that way. I only meant to say . . . Oh, never mind."

Frustrated, she scurried back to the kitchen and began baking.

She baked a loaf of bread on the first day and put it near Gilgamesh's bed. She scratched a mark on the wall to record the first loaf. The next day, she baked another loaf of bread. She marked it on the wall with a second scratch. She did the same thing for seven continuous days. By day seven, the first loaf of bread had become as hard as a rock; the second had become leathery; the third had shrunk to half its original size; the fourth was coated with a white powdery substance; the fifth had begun to display splotches of mold; the sixth had turned stale; and the seventh was still warm from the oven.

It was on day seven that Utnapishtim decided Gilgamesh had slept long enough.

"I've had enough of this," he said. He looked at Old Woman. "Wife, don't try to stop me. He's slept enough." He hobbled up to Gilgamesh and shook him awake with a gentle nudge.

Slowly, Gilgamesh's eyes fluttered open. He yawned. He stretched his arms and legs.

"Where am I?" he asked, looking around the room, disoriented. And then he remembered where he was and why he had come.

"Utnapishtim," he said. "I'm glad to see you. I was just resting my eyes when I felt your touch. I'm ready to take the test now, the one you suggested. What was it again?" he hesitated, collecting his thoughts.

"Oh, yes. Now I remember. You said I should prove myself worthy by staying awake for seven continuous days. I'm ready to start now. I'll show the gods I can rise above my mortal limitations. I'll show them I'm worthy of the gift of everlasting life."

Utnapishtim chuckled.

"I knew it," he said, turning to the old woman. "What did I tell you?"

Old Woman frowned.

"Told her what?" Gilgamesh asked, puzzled. "What's going on?"

"Son, you've been asleep for seven days," Utnapishtim announced, unable to resist a wide grin.

"That's impossible," Gilgamesh said. "I would know if I'd fallen asleep. I didn't sleep at all. How can you say such a thing? Why are you accusing me of sleeping?"

He turned to the woman, seeking her support.

"Why is he accusing me of sleeping? What's going on?"

"Look in front of you, son," Utnapishtim said. "Count the loaves of bread. Wife baked one loaf of bread for each day you were asleep. There are seven loaves in all. The first loaf is as hard as a rock; the second leathery; the third shrank; the fourth powdery; the fifth moldy; the sixth stale; the seventh still warm from the oven. Wife scratched one mark on the wall for each loaf of bread. Count the loaves, son. Count the marks on the wall. Like it or not, son, you've been asleep for seven days."

Utnapishtim sat back in his chair, folding his arms in triumph. He waited.

Gilgamesh's eyes swept across the room. He saw the loaves of bread and counted them slowly. He looked up at Utnapishtim, his eyes wide with disbelief. He took a few steps back, disappointed in himself. How could I? he asked himself. How could I surrender to such a human weakness as the need for sleep? He buried his face in his hands. Tears welled up in his eyes. He tried to choke them back, but he couldn't restrain them. He began to weep uncontrollably.

"Asleep for seven days!" he cried in anguish. "I've lost my strength. What's going to happen to me now? What have I done? Where can I go? I'm no longer strong. I'm weak. I'm as weak as all mortals are weak," he wept.

Old Woman rushed to his side, resting her hand on his shoulder.

"It's all right, son," she said.

"No, it isn't," Gilgamesh cried, his words punctuated by sobs. "Death lurks nearby. I see it everywhere I turn. It sneers at me. It mocks me. I see it in every corner. It prowls behind me. It lies in wait to fasten its grip on me when the gods decree my time is up. I have nowhere to hide. Death will find me. What can I do? Where can I go?" he asked.

His questions tumbled out in desperation, his tone resigned and full of despair.

The woman patted him on the shoulder to comfort him. She felt sorry for the young man, but there was little she could do to ease his despair. Gilgamesh buried his face in his hands and wept pitifully for several minutes. Eventually his tears subsided. He slowly lifted his tear-stained face. He looked at the old woman, his eyes red, his face worn with grief.

"What am I to do?" he pleaded. "Where can I go?"

The woman managed a weak smile. "I think it's best if you go home, son," she suggested, her eyes moist. "You came all this way to hear our story. Now that you have heard it, there's nothing left for you here. You need to go home. Take Siduri's advice. Make the most of what you have. Love your family; show compassion to others; be good to yourself; eat well; and enjoy the life you have. There's nothing else to be done."

Gilgamesh choked back tears. "Have I come all this way for nothing? Am I to die like everyone else? Is this all there is to my life?" he moaned.

"Yes, son," counseled Old Woman. "This is all there is. Your fate is to live and die like all mortals. The quicker you understand this and accept it, the better it will be for you. Do as I say, son. Accept it. Make the most of the life you have left. Heed Siduri's advice and live the rest of your days in harmony with those around you."

Utnapishtim observed the exchange in silence. But his tolerance for Gilgamesh's stubbornness had reached its limits. It's time to put a stop to this nonsense, he thought. The boy needs to face the truth. He needs to grow up. He needs to get off my land and go home. He has no business being here in the first place.

"Urshanabi," he said gruffly. "This young man is filthy. He reeks of sweat and animal flesh. His hair is matted with sand. His body is covered in grime. Prepare a bath for him. Give him a good, thorough scrubbing," he ordered. "He needs it. Wash and comb out his hair. Throw away the soiled animal skins he's been wearing. Dump them into the ocean. Let the waters carry them away. I don't want them to stain this land with their stench.

"Bathe the boy's body. Anoint it with soothing oils. Comb and tie his hair with a colorful headband. Dress him in some of my finest robes. He needs to look like a king instead of a bedraggled boy. Make sure his clothes remain clean on the journey back. He's a king. It's about time he looked and behaved like one instead of a whimpering, filthy little boy."

Urshanabi was surprised by Utnapishtim's orders, delivered with unmistakable anger and impatience. He froze on the spot in a daze, afraid to move. He struggled to digest Utnapishtim's words. Sometimes he was slow to follow orders and slow to move. This was one of those times. He looked at Gilgamesh to see if he showed any signs of being offended by Utnapishtim's harsh words, but Gilgamesh hung his head low, seemingly absorbed with his thoughts elsewhere.

"Do it now, Urshanabi!" Utnapishtim shouted at him from the other side of the room. "I said now! Do it now without talk, without delay."

He shot him a look of frustration and anger.

Urshanabi jumped to attention. Old Woman rushed forward to help. She and Urshanabi heated water on the fireplace and began filling the small tub with warm water. Urshanabi helped Gilgamesh remove the soiled animal skins covering his body. As soon as the tub was ready, Gilgamesh gingerly stepped in and sat down. The water reached up to his chest. Urshanabi scrubbed his body and washed his tangled mass of hair. Old Woman brought towels to dry him. She fetched some of Utnapishtim's finest robes for him to wear.

When he finished bathing Gilgamesh, Urshanabi dried his body and rubbed it generously with oils. He dressed him in one of Utnapishtim's robes, combed his hair, and bound it in a colorful headband. Then he stood back and admired his handy work.

Gilgamesh looked like a new person. His skin was clean and smelled of fragrant oils; his hair was combed and shimmered a deep black as it captured the light. He no longer slouched like a broken man but stood erect with his head held high.

Utnapishtim, too, was pleased with the results.

"That's more like it," he said. "Now you look like a king." He walked up to Gilgamesh and sniffed him. "You even smell like a king," he laughed.

The woman was also pleased. "You look beautiful, son," she exclaimed, grinning from ear to ear.

Utnapishtim's satisfaction was short-lived. Piled on the floor were the discarded animal skins Gilgamesh had worn. His smile turned to a frown as he snapped at Urshanabi.

"Urshanabi, the animal skins! Didn't I tell you to remove them? Why are they still here? Get rid of them at once. I don't want them stinking up the place."

Urshanabi jumped up hurriedly, gathering the animal skins as he spoke. "Sorry, Master," he stuttered. "I was just about to take them down to the beach."

"Well, do it, then," Utnapishtim snarled at him.

Urshanabi grabbed the pile of animal skins and raced down to the beach. Once there, he threw them into the ocean. He watched as the waves swooped in and carried them off. He then walked slowly back up to the house. He was in no hurry to get back. He knew his master was still angry with him. The slightest wrong move on his part and Utnapishtim would unleash a torrent of angry words in his direction. I better be careful, he reminded himself, as he stepped cautiously back into the house.

Gilgamesh, Old Woman, and Utnapishtim were sitting together around the table, talking.

"It's time for you to go, son," she said. "It's time for you to go home."

Gilgamesh nodded.

GILGAMESH OF URUK

Chapter 23: The Expulsion

The woman was pleased to see the change in him. Now that the dirt and grime had been scrubbed off his body, he looked like a new man. He stood erect and proud and beautiful. She could tell he was beginning to brace himself mentally for his journey home.

Utnapishtim gave his final instructions to Urshanabi. "Help him to get home," he said. "He's a king. You must serve him well. Keep his robes clean. Bathe his body regularly on the journey back. Anoint his skin with oils. He must arrive in Uruk looking and feeling like the king he is."

"I understand, Master," Urshanabi said, eager to please.

Utnapishtim paused, his face tense with displeasure. With a determined expression in his eyes, he looked directly at Urshanabi. Old Woman took a deep breath. She knew something was coming.

"And as for you," Utnapishtim said, his voice firm, "because of what you've done, from now on you are forbidden to land on these shores ever again. You're never allowed to cross the waters. You're forbidden to come back here. I am banishing you from this land forever." He paused to let the words register. "Do you understand me, Urshanabi?"

Urshanabi's jaw dropped. His hands began to shake. He obviously had not anticipated this. He looked stunned. Lost. Dilmun was lost to him forever. He didn't know what to say. But he knew his master. Once Utnapishtim had made up his mind, nothing would change it. No one could influence him, except perhaps one person.

Urshanabi looked in her direction. His eyes pleaded with her to say something on his behalf. He needed her

GILGAMESH OF URUK

help. But she shook her head. He was alone in this. He had messed up. He had violated a trust from the gods. There was nothing she could do to help him.

"You must do as Utnapishtim has commanded," she said, looking sternly at Urshanabi.

Urshanabi lowered his eyes and nodded his head. He understood. His fate had been sealed. He knew if Old Woman couldn't help him, no one could.

She saw the look of despair in his eyes, his face downcast and dejected. Once again, her compassion got the better of her. She made her way back into the kitchen and indicated with a nod of her head for him to follow. Urshanabi got up meekly and followed.

"Can't you help me, Mother?" he whispered as soon as he was sure Utnapishtim was out of earshot.

"No."

"But it's such a severe punishment," he pleaded. "I don't deserve this. It wasn't my fault. He threatened to kill me if I didn't bring him here."

"Urshanabi, what did you expect?" She spoke decisively. "You brought this on yourself. You brought a young man to our shores without permission. You showed him how to cross the Waters of Death without the Stone Men. You violated a trust. You angered Utnapishtim. You angered me. And you disregarded the will of the gods. They brought us here to live on this land in seclusion. You can no longer be trusted, Urshanabi."

"But to be banished from this land forever?" Urshanabi said. "To be exiled from Dilmun forever? Mother, it's not fair. It wasn't my fault. What am I to do? Where am I to go? I have nowhere to go. This place is all I know. It's not fair. It wasn't my fault. He's being too hard on me, Mother. Don't you think Utnapishtim is being too hard on me?"

"No, I don't. Honestly, I'm surprised he's letting you off so easily. I think Utnapishtim has been too lenient with you."

"Lenient!" Urshanabi raised his voice.

"Hush! Keep your voice down. Yes, he's been lenient with you," she insisted.

She turned her face hurriedly to see if Utnapishtim had heard anything. But his attention was elsewhere. He was preoccupied with talking to Gilgamesh.

"If it were up to me," she said looking back at Urshanabi, "I would have been a lot more severe with you."

"You would?"

"Most definitely. You committed a serious error in judgment. It's not one that can be easily dismissed or forgotten. I think banishing you from this land is far too lenient a punishment for what you did."

"It is?"

Old Woman paused. She wanted her sentence to sound emphatic and convincing. She wanted to scare him so he wouldn't put up a fuss.

"I would have insisted on your death. I think death is the most suitable punishment for your offense," she said, fixing her eyes firmly on him with an intense stare.

Urshanabi gasped. He couldn't believe the person he called Mother would speak such harsh words. She had always shown him kindness and compassion. She had defended him so many times when Utnapishtim had growled at him with impatience. He couldn't accept the harsh words coming from her mouth. He searched her face for signs of wavering. He stared into her eyes long and hard. She stared back at him, her face frozen in its resolve. He shrugged his shoulders and lowered his eyes.

"Come on, Urshanabi," she said, finally. "Enough of this lingering. We've wasted enough time. The two of you must be off."

She led the way out of the kitchen. Urshanabi followed. They entered in time to hear Utnapishtim speak.

"It's time to go, son," he said, looking at Gilgamesh.

Gilgamesh nodded.

"I know. I'll leave. Thank you for all you've done for me," he added.

He looked at the woman. "Thank you for the kindness you've shown me, Mother," he said.

Old Woman smiled and nodded her head in acknowledgement.

"Come on, son. We'll go down to the shore to see you off," Utnapishtim said.

The four of them walked slowly down the hill toward the boat. Gilgamesh led the way. He walked with his head held high. Urshanabi followed, dragging his feet in the sand. Utnapishtim reached out for his wife's hands. They walked side-by-side, following at a much slower pace.

Urshanabi jumped in as soon as they got to the boat. Gilgamesh followed. They waited for the old man and woman to reach the shore. Urshanabi, too embarrassed to say anything, busied himself with preparing the boat. Gilgamesh gave them a final nod of appreciation. Old Woman smiled and nodded encouragingly. Utnapishtim, a stern expression on his face, was the only one to speak.

"Be on your way, son," he said. "Goodbye."

Urshanabi and Gilgamesh pushed off from the shore and were moving slowly away when the old woman realized something wasn't right, that this wasn't a fitting end to Gilgamesh's adventures.

"Wait!" she shouted. She turned to Utnapishtim with one final request.

"He has come all this way," she said. "Is there nothing you can give him for his return journey home? Surely, there must be something you can give him."

Gilgamesh heard her and maneuvered the boat back to shore, waiting. Utnapishtim hesitated, his brow wrinkled in thought. Finally, he spoke.

"Well, I suppose there is something I can give him."

He faced Gilgamesh.

"Son, you've come a long way, endured many hardships. Like Wife says, it's not right for you to go home empty-handed. I'll give you a precious gift. You must handle it with care for it's a secret revealed to me by the gods. I, alone, know of it. It must be treated with reverence and respect."

Chapter 24: The Plant

Gilgamesh held his breath, afraid to speak. He waited to hear what Utnapishtim had to say.

"There's a plant," he began, "a small, prickly plant. Its sharp spikes will prick your fingers like rose thorns. You must handle it with care or it will make you bleed. This plant carries with it the secret of eternal youth. If you find it, eat its leaves. It will make you young, again. You will lose your fear of death."

"Lose my fear of death? Gilgamesh asked.

"That's right."

"And it will give me eternal youth?"

"Yes."

"What about eternal life? Will it give me eternal life?"

"No, it won't," Utnapishtim replied. "You won't get eternal life. But you will get the next best thing. You will get eternal youth. And, as we both know, young people are unafraid of death. They think they're invincible. They think they'll live forever. Eternal youth will bring with it a loss in your fear of death."

"Where is this plant?" Gilgamesh asked, his voice tense with anticipation. "I must have it. If I can't cheat death, maybe I can delay it indefinitely. I can go back to being young again. I can rid myself of the fear of death. Where can I find this plant?"

"Well, that's the tricky part," Utnapishtim replied. "It's not easy to obtain. It's located way down in the water beneath this sand. It won't be easy to get to it."

"I'm not worried," Gilgamesh bragged. "I can get to it. I'll find it and bring it to the surface." He turned to Urshanabi.

"Urshanabi, help me dig a deep pit."

GILGAMESH OF URUK

The two of them began digging. They dug and dug and dug until they reached an opening that revealed the dark water. Gilgamesh removed his clothes. He tied a heavy stone to each foot. He took a deep breath and plunged into the water. The weight of the stones dragged him further and further down. He held his breath as his eyes scanned the murky darkness. He searched and searched until he found the plant. He grabbed it with both hands and pulled at it. The spikes pricked his fingers. His blood mingled with the waters. Holding the plant with one bloody hand, Gilgamesh used his other hand to untie the stones weighing him down. He floated up to the surface. Clutching the plant with both hands, he gasped for breath.

"I've got it!" he shouted triumphantly. He held the plant up for all to see. Panting heavily, he collapsed on the sand, exhausted.

"Come here, Urshanabi," he said in between gulps of breath. "Come and see this plant. It will restore youth. It will rid us of the fear of death. We might not be able to cheat death. But we can renew our youth and continue to delay it so death can't snatch us."

Urshanabi stepped forward and examined the plant. Its leaves were a dark green, its stem peppered with thorny bristles. It didn't look like a magical plant. It didn't even look very appetizing. Urshanabi doubted such a spindly plant could have any magical properties.

"Aren't you going to test it?" he asked Gilgamesh. "Are you going to eat one of its leaves?"

"No. I'll take it back to Uruk with me. I'll test it by giving it to one of the old men in Uruk. If it restores his youth after he eats one of its leaves, I'll try it myself. I'll be young again. I'll be happy. I won't be afraid of death. I won't be sad. I won't cry." Gilgamesh was elated.

Out of the corner of his eye, Urshanabi could see Utnapishtim getting restless. He helped Gilgamesh put

GILGAMESH OF URUK

on his robes. Gilgamesh clutched the plant tightly with both hands. He gave a parting smile to the elderly couple on the shore. He turned to get on the boat but stopped abruptly. He walked up to the old woman.

"Thank you, Mother."

His dark eyes lingered on her face. His lips turned up into a smile.

Her eyes lit up. She returned his smile, patting him gently on the shoulder.

Gilgamesh got on the boat and he and Urshanabi set off for Uruk.

Utnapishtim and Old Woman stood on the shore. They watched the boat bob gently in the water as Gilgamesh pushed it forward with the oars.

"Do you think he'll be all right?" she asked.

"I don't know. And I don't really care."

"Do you think he's learned anything?"

"I don't know. But somehow I doubt it."

"Why do you think he didn't eat a leaf from the plant?"

"I don't know. Maybe he's afraid of what it might do. Maybe, like he said, he wants to test it on someone else. He wants to see its effects before he has the courage to try it on himself. For all his bluster and bragging, he's still a child in many ways."

"Or maybe once he has seen its magical properties, he will share it with the people of Uruk," Old Woman suggested.

"You think he's that generous?"

"Yes, don't you?"

A wry smile swept across Utnapishtim's face.

"This is the same king who tormented his people in Uruk with his arrogance. The one who oppressed his subjects. The one who intentionally hunted down a creature that posed no threat to him or his people. The one who killed that innocent creature, casually ignoring the poor creature's pleas for mercy and promises to serve him. The one who insulted the goddess Ishtar. The one who killed the Bull of Heaven. The one who strutted about the city doing his little victory dance. The one who demolished the Stone Men in another of his killing rampages."

Utnapishtim paused.

"You seriously think this man is generous enough to share the magical properties of this plant with his people? You think he's capable of showing that kind of consideration?"

Utnapishtim's voice was laced with sarcasm.

"Yes, I do," his wife insisted. "I think he's changed. I think he's learned from his experience. I think he'll go back to Uruk. I think he'll be a just and compassionate king."

Utnapishtim smiled at her. "You always think the best of people."

His eyes twinkled. He smiled, patting her gently on the cheek.

The couple stared at the ocean for several minutes until the boat became a tiny speck on the horizon.

Utnapishtim turned to the woman. He put his arms around her.

"Come on, Wife," he said. "Time to go home. Let's go back to the house. This has been too much excitement for me. I'm tired. Let's go home."

She rested her eyes on his face and smiled. She took his gnarled hand in hers. Together they walked slowly back up to the house.

Chapter 25: The Return

It was unexpected. Neither one was paying attention. They were too busy bathing in a clear pool, refreshing themselves on their journey, washing the grime from their bodies. Gilgamesh carelessly tossed the plant of everlasting youth on the edge of the water. Neither one noticed the snake lurking nearby.

The snake smelled the plant's sweet fragrance. It waited. Gilgamesh was at the far edge of the pool. Urshanabi was distracted. The snake emerged from the water slowly. It slithered up to the plant, snatched it, and carried it off. It shed its old skin as it did so, revealing a new layer of young, healthy looking skin. It plunged back in the water.

Out of the corner of his eye, Gilgamesh saw the snake. "Urshanabi, the plant!"

Urshanabi turned around and plunged at the plant. He was swift, but he wasn't swift enough. The snake slithered away into the water with its prize. The plant was lost forever.

Urshanabi emerged from the water, crestfallen and disappointed. He dried himself off and sat in silence. Gilgamesh slowly maneuvered himself out of the water in a daze. Urshanabi rushed to his side and helped him to dry off, rubbing the oils on his master's body until it glistened in the sun. All the while, he repeated the same phrase over and over again.

"It's all right, Master. It'll be all right. We can go back to Uruk without the plant."

A stunned Gilgamesh, his hopes shattered, sat by the pool's edge and wept. His goal of everlasting life had eluded him. And now he had lost the plant of eternal youth.

"What am I to do?" he sobbed. "I have nothing left, Urshanabi. I have to go back to Uruk empty-handed. It's all been useless."

Urshanabi choked back tears. "It's all right, Master. It'll be all right."

Gilgamesh wiped his tears and sat in silence, deep in thought. Urshanabi hesitated to disturb him. Eventually he got up and the two of them resumed their journey. They spoke little, Urshanabi engrossed with worries about what the future held for him in the city of Uruk, and Gilgamesh struggling to come to terms with his loss.

After traveling many miles, they arrived in Uruk. Gilgamesh approached the city with a renewed vigor, glowing with pride. He swaggered on top of the wall surrounding the city.

"See this wall of Uruk, Urshanabi. I built it."

His face beamed.

"Look at how the brickwork shines in the sun like copper."

Urshanabi stared in amazement. The wall seemed to stretch for miles and miles around the city.

"Come up here to the top of the wall," Gilgamesh invited him. "Climb up the stone staircase and examine it closely. See how impressive it is. And, look," he said pointing straight ahead. "There's the Eanna Temple of the goddess Ishtar. There's no other temple like it for its size and beauty."

Urshanabi's eyes swept in the direction Gilgamesh indicated. Before him stood the temple dedicated to the goddess Ishtar. Urshanabi gasped. He had never seen a structure so magnificent. The outside walls of the temple were covered with turquoise, yellow, and dark blue mosaics. The yellow mosaics glistened like gold in the sunlight. The lapis lazuli mosaics added sheen and luster. Images of bulls and antelopes framed with geometric patterns of mosaics lined up at regular intervals on the wall.

Urshanabi's gaze turned to the temple door, at least ten times the height of a man and dwarfing humans by its size. He had never seen anything like it. Leading up to the door was a path of red bricks, glistening in the sun. Urshanabi held his breath. No wonder Gilgamesh spoke with such pride of his city, he thought.

"Is this where the sacred priestesses reside?" he asked, remembering Gilgamesh's story of Shamhat and the role of the goddess Ishtar's sacred priestesses.

Gilgamesh laughed. "Yes, Urshanabi. This is where they reside." He strutted up and down on the city wall as he spoke.

"Look here, Urshanabi," he said, pointing in the other direction. "Look at the gardens. See the palm trees with their clusters of dates, the flowers in every color you can imagine. See the orchards laden with figs and grapes and oranges and apples."

Urshanabi followed Gilgamesh's gaze. His eyes grew wide in astonishment. Never had he beheld such plush gardens with so many fruits and flowers. He feasted his eyes on the splendor. And then something strange caught his eye. It looked like a very large brown snake circling its way through the city.

"What's that?" he asked.

"That's the canal," Gilgamesh replied.

"Canal?" Urshanabi asked. He had never before heard of a canal. "What's a canal?"

"The canal is the system we've built to make the water flow throughout the city."

Gilgamesh glowed with pride.

"It's wonderful, isn't it? It connects us with the Euphrates River, making it easy for us to trade goods with our neighbors. And it lets us water our soil so crops can grow."

Urshanabi was astonished. He had never heard of such a system. "You mean you can make the water come to you?" he asked.

"Yes, Urshanabi. We can make the water come to us." Gilgamesh grinned.

Urshanabi's jaw dropped. All he could do was stare in wonder.

"And look down here," Gilgamesh said, pointing below. "Look at the market place bustling with commerce. Look at the homes with their welcoming courtyards and entryways. Look at the public squares with their open spaces for people to gather. Isn't it beautiful? Doesn't it take your breath away? Isn't this the most beautiful city you've ever seen?"

Gilgamesh flushed with pleasure.

Urshanabi looked down and gasped. So many people all in one place! This is a huge city, he thought. How can they all be living together like this, he wondered. He wasn't used to seeing so many people clumped together at the same time. He scrunched up his face to observe their movements carefully. They seemed to be comfortable jostling in the crowd, talking and laughing with each other, and haggling with merchants. The city was abuzz with activity. Perhaps they're used to the throngs of people, he thought. He wasn't sure he would ever get used to living among so many people, no matter how beautiful the city.

Gilgamesh noticed the worried look on Urshanabi's face.

"Look at the people, Urshanabi," he said. "See the women? What did I tell you? Aren't they the most beautiful women you've ever seen? They're dressed in colorful gowns of blues and greens and yellows and reds and purples. I'll bet you've never seen embroidery so delicate and intricate as the embroidery on their headdresses and cloaks. What did I tell you? Isn't this the most beautiful city in the world? Aren't you happy to be here?"

Urshanabi nodded in agreement. The women were, indeed, very beautiful. He had never seen such beautiful women or so many of them in one place. He had never seen a city like Uruk. Maybe I could get used to this after all, he said to himself.

Gilgamesh paused to feast his eyes on the splendor. He took a deep breath.

"It's so good to be home."

He clambered off the wall and entered the city. The people of Uruk immediately surrounded him. They greeted him as a returning hero. They celebrated his return by circling dances around him and Urshanabi, playing music, and singing in his honor. Gilgamesh was finally home.

And as it turned out, Old Woman had been right, after all.

When the festivities subsided, Gilgamesh shared the story of his grueling journey to Utnapishtim the Faraway. He told his subjects how Utnapishtim had survived the flood. He taught them how to perform the ancient rites they had long since abandoned. He stopped tormenting his people. He was just, compassionate, and understanding. The Gilgamesh who returned from his epic journey was no longer the same Gilgamesh who had set off.

Gilgamesh ruled Uruk for many years. When he died, his wife, son, and the city of Uruk mourned his loss for many days. They sang his praises. They offered gifts to the gods to accept Gilgamesh in their midst. The elders recorded his story on clay tablets.

He lived over 4,000 years ago. He loved Enkidu. He killed Humbaba of the Cedar Forest. He killed the Bull of Heaven. He built the city wall. He went on a long journey to find Utnapishtim the Faraway. He brought back the story of the flood. He ruled his people with compassion. He was a great king. He wanted his name to be remembered forever. His wish came true.

His name was Gilgamesh, King of Uruk

ALSO AVAILABLE BY TAMARA AGHA-JAFFAR

Unsung Odysseys
Odysseus' ten-year journey home from Troy is explored through the multiple voices of the women embroiled in his adventures—a distraught mother, a patient wife, a devoted nurse, a benevolent witch, a possessive nymph, a lovesick princess, and a loyal goddess.
Their silence has finally been broken in words that vibrate with heartfelt clarity and timeless messages.

A Pomegranate and the Maiden
A multi-faceted re-telling of the story of Demeter and Persephone as told in Homer's *Hymn to Demeter*. The many characters speak directly to the reader, presenting multiple perspective of the same event. Among the voices we hear is that of the mother grieving for her lost child, the daughter struggling for independence, the father trampling on a mother's rights, and the lover resorting to nefarious means to win his beloved. Each perspective is deeply rooted in the character's psychology and gender. Woven within their narratives are stories familiar to readers of Greek mythology.

Women and Goddesses in Myth and Sacred Text
A multi-cultural anthology of primary texts examining the role of major female figures in Western and non-Western religions and mythologies. Key texts from a variety of cultures offer insight into the women and goddesses honored by contemporary world religions and indigenous traditions.
The text features questions for critical reading to accompany each primary selection; a balanced coverage

to compare and contrast different traditions; a glossary of names and terms to precede each primary reading; and suggestions for further reading.

Demeter and Persephone: Lessons From a Myth
Analysis and discussion of the Demeter/Persephone myth that illustrates its continued importance and relevance. The work explores the mother/daughter relationship; the symbolism of critical objects; female mentoring; the masculinist perspective presented by Zeus and Hades; a psychological interpretation of the underworld; and lessons on healing.

The *Hymn to Demeter* as translated by Helen Foley is included in the Appendix. Notes and a bibliography follow the text.

www.tamaraaghajaffar.com

Printed in Great Britain
by Amazon